THE CAT STOLE
MY PANTS

Praise for the series

TiMMY FAILURE

THE CAT STOLE
MY PANTS

Stephan Pastis

WALKER
BOOKS

First published in Great Britain 2017 by Walker Books Ltd
87 Vauxhall Walk, London SE11 5HJ

This edition published 2019

4 6 8 10 9 7 5 3

This book has been typeset in Nimrod

Printed and bound by CPI Group (UK) Ltd, Croydon CR0 4YY

British Library Cataloguing in Publication Data:
a catalogue record for this book is available from the British Library

ISBN 978-1-4063-9562-4

www.walker.co.uk

www.timmyfailure.com

A Prologue That Time-wise Would Take Place Somewhere Between Chapters 39 and 40 But Which Is Being Presented to You Now Instead Because It's Quite Dramatic and Compelling

A six-toed cat stole my pants.

On an island called Key West in Florida.

ROUND
ABOUT
HERE

FLORIDA

It happened when we were touring the house of a famous author.

Who I know nothing about.

Other than that he is dead.

So when my mother made me dress up for the tour, I knew it wasn't to impress *him*.

Me
(impressing
no one)

I also didn't know that the interior of the dead guy's house would have no air-conditioning. Causing me to sweat so profusely as to be medically unsafe.

Which is probably what killed the author.

But I am the detective Timmy Failure.

And I am harder to kill than an author.

So when the heat of the house becomes overwhelming, I leave my mother with the tour group and walk back outside.

Where I do what any sane person would do.

And remove my pants.

← Me (This time with no pants)

But my cool pants-less respite is cut short by the sound of my mother's voice calling to me from the upstairs windows of the house.

"Timmy? Where are you? *Timmy?*"

So I grudgingly return inside and stand amidst the tour group.

"What do you think you're doing?" she whispers, pulling me to the back of the group.

"Saving my life," I answer. "So I don't end up like the dead guy."

I point toward the author's picture on the wall.

The dead guy ←

"Timmy, you are standing in a public place in your underwear."

"It's my Mr. Froggie underwear. So people will think it's a fancy bathing suit. And besides, why do I have to dress up anyway? Everyone else here is in shorts."

Before she can say anything else, we are

interrupted by the old man who is our tour guide.

"Folks, next we're gonna go see the room where Mr. Hemingway wrote."

"I don't know who that is," I reply as I shuffle past him in my underwear.

"Ernest Hemingway. You're standing in his house," he says, then pauses. "You're standing *in your underwear* in his house. Son, could you please put on some pants?"

"I am so sorry," says my overly apologetic mother as she rushes me out of the upstairs bedroom we are in and onto the wraparound verandah.

"Timmy, where did you leave them?"

"Who knows? Maybe next to the fountain outside. The one the cats were drinking out of."

"You stay here," she tells me. "Don't move."

So I stand outside on the verandah beneath a large ceiling fan and stare at the pudgy tourists below.

And that's when I see him.
The cat with six toes.

"Polydactyl," says the tour guide, peer-
ing out of the double doors that lead onto the

verandah. "That means he has more than the usual number of toes. Like the kind of cat that Papa owned."

"They're like giant mittens," I reply. "And who the heck is Papa?"

"Ernest 'Papa' Hemingway," he says. "Or 'the dead guy,' as you call him."

And as he says it, I hear my mother's footsteps rushing back toward us on the verandah. "Your pants are not on the fountain, Timmy. They're not *anywhere*."

"Of course they're not," I reply. "Because they've been stolen."

"Stolen?" she says. "Who would steal pants?"

"Him," I say.

"The cat," she says.

"Yes," I answer. "With giant mittens for paws. Could walk off with half the furniture in this house if he wanted to."

"Timmy, that little cat does not steal pants."

"He's never stolen *my* pants," the tour guide interjects. "And I've been here fifteen years."

The tour guide smiles at my mother. She does not smile back. He slinks back inside the bedroom and rejoins the departing tour group.

"Timmy, I want you to focus. Where did you see them last?"

"I told you already. By the fountain."

"Yeah, well, *as I told you* already, they're not there."

"So talk to Mr. Mittens over there," I answer, pointing again at the cat. "It's a genetic mutation. We learned about it in science. God or Charlie Darwinian or somebody gave that little cat a thumb so he can grab things. And unfortunately for us, he has chosen to use that skill for evil ends. Namely, the theft of my pants."

Mr. Mittens meows.

"Cats do not wear pants," my mother answers in that unique motherly tone that is half whisper and half scream.

"Correct," I answer. "Which is why he probably sold them on the kitty black market."

She opens her mouth to once again lecture me but is stopped short by a man's voice.

This one from beneath the verandah.

"Are you guys gonna come down here or just stay up there talking all day?"

So my mother peers over the railing.

"Tell that nosy tour guide to mind his own business," I say to her.

My mother looks back at me, and suddenly, the anger is drained from her face, replaced by something else.

It is as though she has seen the error of her ways, perhaps owing to a glimpse of Mr. Mittens absconding with my pants.

"It's not the tour guide," she says.

"Is it a cat wearing pants?" I answer.

She shakes her head and reaches out her hand to take mine, pulling me toward the railing.

Where I peer down at the man. Who I don't recognize.

"Papa," she says.

I stare back inside at the picture of the white-bearded man on the wall, and then back toward the younger man beneath the verandah.

And they look nothing alike.

"Not the writer," she says, reading my thoughts.

Pausing briefly to squeeze my hand.

"It's your father."

CHAPTER
1

Give Me Your Timmy, Your Poor, Your Huddled Masses

Many years ago, a zillion desperate people—all seeking a better life—escaped from a country called Cuba to a place called Key West, Florida. Many years later, one desperate boy—also seeking a better life—escaped from Key West, Florida, to Cuba.

"Timmy, get back here so I can put lotion on you," says my mother.

"I'm almost to Cuba," I answer.

"You're two feet from the shore," she says. "In Florida."

"Google says that Cuba is only ninety miles away. I can swim that in an hour. And if I don't like it, I'll swim right back."

"Timmy," she says, yanking me out of the water by my arm and slathering sunscreen across my face, "I want you to come back to where we are on the beach, and I want you to play with Emilio. The poor kid's just standing up there waving at you."

"But look at him, Mother. Wearing his little ducky thing. It's embarrassing."

"It's not embarrassing, Timmy. Stop making life difficult."

"Well, I didn't want to come to stupid Key West in the first place."

"What did you want us to do? Leave you at home? Leave you for a week with some baby-sitter we barely know?"

"Yes," I answer.

"No," she snaps back. "Dave and I would have just worried about you. That would have ruined our entire honeymoon."

Honeymoon.

A word that the Merriam-Webster diction-ary defines suchly:

> # HONEYMOON, *noun*
>
> 1) a pleasant period of time at the start of something, such as a relationship
>
> 2) a trip or vacation taken by a newly married couple

Which reminds me.

The first thing I'm going to do when I get off this remote island is write to Mr. Merriam or Mr. Webster or Mr. Merriam-Webster and tell them all to update their stupid dictionary.

Because:

1) This trip is a far cry from pleasant; and

2) My mother is not married.

Well, *she* would say she is married. But there is no proof.

Because somebody named me fainted during the ceremony.

A LOOK BACK

And so I witnessed none of the unpleasantness.

Which brings me to the whole Emilio thing.

Emilio is the nephew of my mother's so-called "husband," Doorman Dave.

Doorman Dave was once our doorman.

But then my mother decided to marry him. So now Doorman Dave is So-Called Husband Dave.

And Emilio is here because—well, I'll just let my mother explain that one:

"We thought it'd be nice for you to have a playmate."

A playmate.

As though I'm a toddler sipping milk through a swirly straw while stacking my alphabet blocks.

And my mother's comment is made doubly offensive by the fact that I *already have* a companion.

My former business partner, Total.

Who is a polar bear.

And a fast swimmer.

And is by now already in Cuba.

CHAPTER 2

X Marks the Tot

"I am the founder, president, and CEO of Failure, Inc., the best detective agency in the town, probably the country, perhaps the world," I tell Emilio. "Write that part down."

Emilio writes it down.

"How many detective agencies *are* there in the world?" he asks.

"What does that matter?" I answer.

"Well, how do you know if you're the greatest if you don't know how many there are?"

I reach over and draw an X in Emilio's notebook.

"What's that?" he asks.

"A demerit. You'll get one demerit every time you ask an inappropriate question."

Emilio writes that down, too.

"And you will be my intern."

"How much does that pay?" asks Emilio.

"It doesn't. So technically, you will be my *unpaid* intern."

"But why should I do it for nothing?"

I glare at Emilio. He writes an X in his notebook.

I pace the long wooden dock we are standing on. At the end of it is a gazebo that now serves as the temporary global headquarters of Failure, Inc.

FAILURE, INC.
TEMPORARY
GLOBAL
HEADQUARTERS

"Emilio—" I pause. "What is your last name, Emilio?"

"Empanada."

"Isn't that a food?" I inquire.

"Yes," he says. "They're quite tasty."

EMPANADA
(TASTY)

MEAT
INSIDE

"Emilio Empanada," I continue. "You will not be doing this for the money. Because money comes and goes."

He writes that down.

"You will be doing it for the glory. Because glory lasts forever."

GLORIOUS POSE

A tear rolls down his cheek.

"I see you're moved to tears," I tell him. "That is not an uncommon reaction."

"No," he says as he rubs his eye. "I wear contact lenses. And I just got sand behind the lens."

I ignore the emotional Emilio Empanada and continue.

"Normally, I would not hire someone as inexperienced and emotional as yourself. But being that I am stuck with you, through no fault of my own, I have chosen to make the best of it."

He raises his hand.

"Yes, Emilio Empanada?"

"I overheard you saying something to your mother about a polar bear. Why is that?"

I remove a torn piece of notebook paper from my pocket.

"Yes," I answer. "His name is Total. And everything you need to know on that subject is in this document. Do not share it with anyone."

Emilio reviews the confidential document.

"You have a polar bear who eats people?" he asks.

"Yes," I answer. "And given your last name, you'll be especially vulnerable."

"I'm bigger than an empanada."

"Size is relative to a polar bear," I explain.

He doesn't write that down.

"Now you'll need detective supplies," I explain to him. "Like secret microphones and brass knuckles and fingerprint kits. And you'll need a bulletproof vest."

He doesn't write that down, either.

"Why aren't you taking notes?" I ask.

"I'm just wondering," he says, scratching his head. "Where *is* this polar bear? Because I don't see him."

I point past the end of the dock toward the aqua sea that stretches to the horizon. "Somewhere out that way. He is seeking political asylum in Cuba."

"I don't know what that means," says Emilio.

"You don't have to. All you need to know is that he is seeking a better life. And if you ever see a fifteen-hundred-pound furry beast arrive back on these shores, you are to run as though your life depended on it. Because it does."

Emilio stares at me, shielding his eyes from the sun.

"What now?" I ask.

"I don't believe that you really have a polar bear. I think that you're just making that part up."

I grab the notebook from his hands and make an X on every one of the remaining pages.

"And you'll need a new notebook," I tell him.

CHAPTER
3
Cleanliness Is Next to Annoyingness

"I can't work with him," I tell my mother on the porch of our rented Key West home.

"It's only for a week," she says.

"He asks inappropriate questions. He has no respect for the detective business. And he fails to understand the reclusive nature of polar bears."

"You'll just have to teach him all those things."

"Teach him? He barely understands that he's an intern. An *unpaid* intern!"

"Not so loud, Timmy."

"Why? Where is he?"

"Inside. He's taking a shower."

"And that's another thing," I add. "That's like his third shower today."

"Well, it's hot here. Maybe he sweats a lot."

"And why does he hang his pants on a hanger?"

"Maybe he doesn't want to wrinkle them."

"And while we're at it, why does he have to tuck a stupid napkin into the top of his shirt when he eats? It's absurd."

"Maybe he likes to be neat. Or maybe he just has nice manners."

"Yeah, well, he's in the wrong business, then. Detectives pride themselves on getting their hands dirty and having *lousy* manners."

"Timmy, Emilio is not a detective."

"You're right. And now he's not even an intern. Because I just decided to fire him."

"You can't fire somebody you don't actually employ."

"Fine. Are we on an island?"

"Yes."

"Then I'm voting him off the island."

"Good timing!" says Doorman Dave, poking his head onto the porch.

"What's good timing?" I ask.

"Voting someone off the island," he answers. "Because today we're *all* getting off the island."

"We're going home!" I shout with joy.

"Nope," he answers. "We're going fishing!"

CHAPTER
4
Worming My Way Out

If you ever want to know what it's like to go fishing on a boat for $200 a person, just do the following:

1) Grab the sides of a toilet and throw up; and

2) Set fire to $200.

Because that is how I have been spending my day fishing with Doorman Dave.

It is a waste of money so profound as to be almost criminally negligent.

And if you're wondering why I didn't mention Emilio Empanada, that is because he's not here.

And why?

Because as we were leaving our rented home, Emilio dramatically announced that he was getting "sniffly" and feared that if he went out on the boat, his cold would get worse.

So he is at home reading.

And as if that's not offensive enough, consider this:

He is reading a *romance* novel.

And because Emilio Empanada couldn't go fishing, that meant my mother couldn't go fishing. Because *someone* had to take care of Doorman Dave's nephew.

And thus, an afternoon of maritime bonding with Doorman Dave ensued.

Which, it must be said, was tragic from the outset.

"Just grab the little worm with one hand and grab the hook with the other."

"Detectives do not touch worms, Dave."

And with that, he thrust the worm in front of my face. Where it could have easily inflicted a fatal wound.

Which would have given the book you are holding a very abrupt ending.

> ### And Timmy died.
>
> ## THE END

So I did what any detective with lightning-quick reflexes would do when confronted by a lethal foe.

I tumbled backward over the side of the boat.

"Happy?" I ask Doorman Dave as he pulls me back into the boat. "You've ruined my custom-made scarf. I suppose you will be making a call to Lazar's of New York to order another?"

"Your scarf will be fine."

"My scarf will not be fine," I correct him. "And neither will I. For now hypothermia has set in. Please, if your goal is to end my once-promising life, say so now and cast me adrift upon the Gulf Stream."

Dave tries to dry me off with a beach towel.

But it is useless.

For I am dying.

"Are you cold?" asks a grizzled voice from inside the bridge of the ship.

I turn and see the captain.

"Yes," I reply. "I am dying."

"Then come in here for a while and warm up. I have a space heater. And maybe if you recover, I'll let you steer the ship."

And with that, my nautical career begins.

The Young Man and the Sea

Dear Total,

Ahoy.

I am now a sea captain.

As such, I intend to sail to Cuba and rescue ye.

That is, if ye wish to be rescued. For at this point, I do not know if ye are stranded on a Cuban beach...
HELP

Things here are desperate.
Yours at Sea,
Pirate Timmy
Yaargggggh

CHAPTER
6
A Pizza Fork in the Road

"I steered the ship the entire way back to port," I tell Doorman Dave as we disembark.

"Well, you steered for about a minute and then threw up on the captain."

"Yes, well, the pressures of running a ship are immense. I wouldn't expect a recreational fisherman to understand."

"I see," says Dave. "Well, the important thing is that we got to spend time together."

"I wouldn't get used to that, Dave."

"No?"

"No. Because for me, it's career first. And as you've saddled me with a particularly unqualified intern, the week ahead will be especially trying."

Dave puts his hand on my shoulder as we begin the short walk home.

"Be nice to Emilio. He likes you."

"He's an employee, Dave. Or more like a former employee. I'm thinking about firing him."

Dave smiles.

"What you do with your detective agency is up to you, Timmy."

"Yes, Dave. I know that."

"But you have to know a couple of things about Emilio."

"Let me guess. He irons his socks."

"No," answers Dave.

"Eats pizza with a fork?" I ask.

"No. Timmy, listen. It's a little more serious than that."

"More serious than eating pizza with a fork? This I have to hear."

"Well, first off," says Dave, "he has no siblings."

"No siblings? *I* don't have any siblings. And look how well I've turned out."

Dave rubs his chin.

"Yes, Timmy, but there's a bit more to it than that," he says as we turn up the front walkway to our house.

"Good, because so far, it sounds like a charmed life."

"Okay, let me start over," says Doorman Dave.

But there is no time for that.

Because Abraham Lincoln is calling.

CHAPTER 7

The Unanticipated Proclamation

I run up the front steps of our house and pick up the phone.

"Hello?"

"Timmy, it's me, Rollo! Summer school is great! We have Mr. Jenkins! And he's teaching American history! I can't believe you're not here. We're even having a play, and guess who I get to be."

"How did you get this number?" I ask my best friend, Rollo Tookus.

ROLLO TOOKUS (As normally attired.)

Stanfurd

"You gave it to me," he says.

"For emergencies," I reply. "Not for telling me about stupid school plays."

"All right, well, just guess who I'm gonna be."

"No."

"Abraham Lincoln!" he shouts. "I get to recite the Emancipation Proclamation!"

"Good for you, Rollo. But I'm bored already."

"Bored? Theater is exciting!"

"Maybe for you. But for me, steering a ship is exciting. Saving the lives of hundreds of people is exciting. All of which I just did."

"You mean like pretend?"

"No, Rollo. For real. Thirty-foot waves. Perilous reefs. I'd tell you more, but I think I have scurvy."

"Scurvy? That's from not getting enough vitamin C."

"Correct."

"Are there no stores where you are where you can get some orange juice? I thought Key West was a fancy vacation place."

"No, Rollo. Key West is the edge of a frontier. Things here are stark. Uncivilized. Lawless. You may never see me again."

"So you're not gonna come to summer school when you get back?"

"Summer school?!" I shout to Abraham Lincoln. "Summer school is for people without lives. I'm a sea captain. I *save* lives."

"Well, that's odd, then."

"What's odd?" I ask.

And that's when Abraham Lincoln delivers the worst news since the Battle of Bull Run.

"The teacher said your name in roll call."

CHAPTER
8
Timmy's Death in the Afternoon

"You did what?" I yell at my mother as I walk into the kitchen.

"I thought you'd *want* to go to summer school. Your friends are all there. It could be fun."

I am so upset I am speechless.

So I draw her a diagram.

"Oh, here we go with the Mr. Dramatic stuff again," says my mother.

"Mr. Dramatic?" I fire back. "First off, how am I even supposed *to take* a class? I'm not even there."

"Timmy, you're only missing a week of class. And I asked Rollo's mom to e-mail me this week's assignments."

"Homework? During summer vacation? You can't do this! I have an upset stomach! Hypothermia! Scurvy!"

She reaches into the refrigerator and pours me a glass of orange juice. "Drink this," she says. "You'll be fine."

So I choose the only sensible option remaining for a child facing summer school.

And fake my own death.

CHAPTER 9

Timmy and Rufus and Doris and Emilio

"'Look into my eyes, Doris,' said the man with the strong chin. 'I will take you to places of the heart that you've never been.'

'Oh, Rufus,' she replied. 'Take me. I am yours.'

'No, Doris, you take me.'

'No, Rufus, you take me.'

*Unable to decide who should take whom,
Doris and Rufus ate a pizza."*

I am lying in bed.

And Emilio Empanada is reading me
romance novels.

For in an evil counterstroke, my mother
used my fake death as an excuse to stick me
in a room with the sniffly Emilio Empanada,
lover of romance novels.

And my sarcastic mother even made a
sign.

Emilio stops reading and sets the book down on his lap.

"Isn't it beautiful?" he asks. "The love between Doris and Rufus?"

"It's absurd," I answer. "Rufus is a bag of useless platitudes. And Doris is not much better."

"I think you're missing the subtle under-tones of this literature," says Emilio. "But that's okay. I can read you *Love Is a Speckled Pony of Desire* instead."

"No, thanks, Emilio. That sounds even worse. I'm only lying in bed because my mother made me."

"What about *The Looming Milk Maiden of Love*?" asks Emilio. "It has a good ending."

"I told you, Emilio. I don't want to hear any more of your literature."

"How about if I just skip to the end?"

"No."

But he flips to the end anyway.

And when he gets there, a piece of paper flutters to the ground.

And it is not about Doris or Rufus.

CHAPTER 10
Kapok Fear

"My life is in grave danger!" I shout to Emilio Empanada. "We must act!"

So I jump out the window.

COOL ACTION-HERO MOVE →

And slide down the balcony support.

And find my intern on the front porch.

And we run.

From palm tree to palm tree.

Avoiding assassins.

"But why would somebody threaten you?" Emilio asks me as we flee.

"Because they know my reputation as a detective. And they don't want me here."

"So what do we do?"

"Survey the entire island. Find out what we're up against."

"And how do we do that?" he asks, panting harder with each step.

"We rent a seaplane. I'll fly it. You just hang on."

"That seems dangerous," says Emilio.

"For normal people," I tell him. "But I'm not normal people."

Emilio nods as he runs.

"But do you even know how to fly a seaplane?" he adds, almost breathless.

"No. But I've captained a ship. And they're identical tasks."

We come to a bizarre native tree and hide behind its strange tall roots.

"We can shelter here," I announce. "Give you a chance to catch your breath. You appear to be in no shape for detective work."

"I'm not," he says.

"What is this thing, anyway?" I ask, staring up at the unusual tree.

"A kapok tree," says Emilio.

"How do you know that?"

"That's a demerit," I inform Emilio. "Never attempt to show up your boss."

He makes an X in his notebook.

"Especially when you are an unpaid intern," I add.

He makes two X's in his notebook.

"Speaking of working for you," Emilio says, looking up from his notebook, "I think it would be bad to be maimed in my first week. So I vote we do something other than fly."

I glance at him.

"Not that I'm afraid," he adds.

"Fear is a cruel master," I inform Emilio Empanada. "Best to overcome it now, while you're still an unpaid intern."

"I see," says Emilio. "Well, maybe later."

"Fine. I shall be merciful and select another option. But next time we fly."

And leaping up from the shelter of the kapok tree, I lead him to the most strategic spot on the island.

CHAPTER
11
You Lighthouse Up My Life

"How'd you know this was here?" asks Emilio.

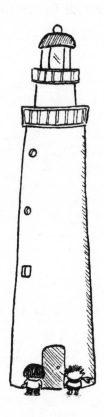

"I spotted it from the bow of my sailing vessel," I answer. "When you were at home sniffling."

Emilio stares at the top of the lighthouse. "I bet from the top of that we can see everything!"

"Yes," I reply. "And if we hurry, we may even spot the person who wrote that note. They're probably fleeing as we speak."

So we rush toward the lighthouse door.

And are stopped by a potbellied man.

"Five bucks for each of you," says the man, his fingers steeped in a carton of greasy conch fritters.

"Police business," I announce. "We are in hot pursuit."

"Five bucks," he says. "Each."

"But we don't have any money," adds Emilio.

"Then I guess you can't go in the lighthouse," he says, popping another fritter in his mouth.

"You'd prefer to have a felon escape our grasp?" I ask.

"I'd prefer to not be fired for letting two kids get in without paying."

"That does it," I announce. "I want your badge number."

"You want my what?"

"Badge number," I repeat. "The number on your badge there. I will be reporting you to the authorities for hindering a police investigation."

"My badge just says 'Larry,'" he answers. "So I guess my badge number is Larry."

I contemplate tackling him. Or stealing his conch fritters.

When I am attacked by a bird of prey.

CHAPTER 12

A Moveable Chicken Feast

"It's not a bird of prey," says Lighthouse Larry. "It's a chicken."

"Chickens kill millions of people every year," I inform him informatively.

"Nope," he says. "Chickens are harmless."

"Emilio, when we get back home, research chicken homicides. I want statistics."

I brush myself off and nobly stand.

"Sir, you leave me no choice but to sue you in a court of law."

"You think a lawyer will take your case?" asks Lighthouse Larry.

"Of course," I answer, then turn to my unpaid intern. "Emilio, when we get home, look up all the lawyers in Key West that handle chicken attack cases. We are going to sue the pants off Lighthouse Larry here."

"I don't wear pants," says Larry, citing a legal technicality. "I wear shorts."

SHORTS
(THUS, CAN'T BE SUED.)

Recognizing the strength of his argument, I offer to compromise.

"In that case, sir, I offer to settle the matter out of court for a reasonable sum. I'll open the bidding at $63,000,000 dollars."

"That's a very specific amount," says Lighthouse Larry.

"It's the total cost of opening detective offices throughout Spain and India. I'm expanding my business rapidly."

"So you're a detective?"

"Yes. I am Failure. Timmy Failure. As if you don't recognize me."

"Well, then, Mr. Failure, as a detective, maybe you should know that there are chickens and roosters roaming all over Key West. And they're not mine. They're just here."

"Good God," I mutter. "How dangerous *is* this lawless island?"

"Not dangerous at all," says Lighthouse Larry. "As far as I know, you're the only person who's ever fallen to the ground and threatened to sue when a chicken brushed past his leg."

"Fine. Then I shall offer once again to compromise. In lieu of $63,000,000, I shall accept free admission to the lighthouse for my intern and myself. A ten-dollar value. And a reduction of $62,999,990 from my last offer."

"No," says Lighthouse Larry.

"You, sir, are an outrageous affront to the legal system. I know my rights."

"Good. Then have you thought about suing the chicken?"

I ponder that.

Chickens *are* arrogant.

And they need to be taught a lesson: Stay away from humans. We have rights.

So I turn to my intern for assistance.

And he is feeding a chicken.

CHAPTER
13
Chickens and Roosters and Bears—Oh, My!

We are followed home by every chicken and rooster on the island of Key West.

"Now look what you've done," I inform my unpaid intern.

"I didn't know they'd follow us," says Emilio.

"Yes, well, they have. And the important thing now is to not show fear. That's when they pounce."

"Why would they pounce?"

"To take our wallets."

But as soon as we get to our rented home, there is a loud squawk from one of the chickens and an abrupt flapping of wings. And in an instant, all of the birds are running in every direction.

And when I look back upon the verandah of our house, I see why.

CHAPTER 14

Protection Against the Elements

The return of my furry Arctic friend is an unexpected development. For he has not communicated with me since his hasty flight to Cuba.

I examine his person to determine if he has been starved or mistreated by his Cuban hosts.

But he is fatter than ever.

And chomping on a Cuban cigar.

"Surely you've returned because you've heard about the vicious threats upon my person," I tell Total. "Well, the rumors are true. I've been threatened. And my life is hanging by a proverbial thread."

Clearly stunned, Total says nothing.

"Just know this," I assure my former business partner. "I am in no way afraid. Though I *am* concerned that my unpaid intern may not have the physical capacity to protect me against gangs of roving assassins."

I look around for Emilio Empanada.

And find him singing a lullaby to a chicken.

ROCK-A-BYE
CHICKEN,
IN THE
TREETOP...

I return to my polar bear.

"Thusly, I've decided to bring you back into Failure, Inc.," I tell Total as I pace the verandah. "Not as a named partner, or even a partner, but as a corporate bodyguard. Muscle, if you will. Your job will be to preserve my life against all threats, foreign and domestic. You'll receive health benefits and perhaps even dental coverage."

I stop pacing and turn back to look at him.

But he is not there.

It is then that I hear his large girth bounding down our home's old wooden staircase, like tropical thunder ripping through the Keys.

And when he re-emerges onto the verandah, he is holding a large bottle of SPF 100 sunscreen.

"You swam all the way back from Cuba because you forgot your suntan lotion?!" I shout.

He nods as he slathers the suntan lotion all over his furry shoulders.

And before I can say another word, he is galloping down the street and onto the beach and into the blue-green waters of the Gulf.

Angry, I yell out to his departing silhouette.

"I hope it's not waterproof!"

CHAPTER 15

The People Who Knew Too Little

Bereft of my polar bear's protection, I realize I have precious few hours to live. I must find my nemesis before he finds me or risk the end of my once-promising life.

But manhunts are expensive.

And I am short of even the ten dollars I need to climb to the top of the lighthouse.

So I put my detective mind to work, and within minutes, I have the solution.

"We will sell this to the masses," I announce, holding a sheaf of papers overhead. "And we will make millions. Perhaps billions."

"What is it?" asks Emilio Empanada, looking up from his book, *The Flame of the Fireman's Desire*.

"I am calling it *Timmy Failure's Wisdom-Filled Guide for the Uneducated People Who Don't Know Very Much*."

"Hmm," says my unpaid intern. "Maybe we should work a little more on the title."

"The title's not important. The point is what's *inside* the book."

"And what's that?" asks Emilio.

"Scenarios that test your detective skills. Each one is multiple choice."

"What kind of scenarios?" asks Emilio.

"Here," I say, handing him my master-piece. "You may read it for free."

(Note from Timmy: As a bonus to you, the reader, I am excerpting parts of the book here. You do not have to pay extra for it at this time. But if you do read it and gain wisdom, please post me a cheque for $1,000.)

<u>Timmy Failure's Wisdom-Filled Guide for the Uneducated People Who Don't Know Very Much</u>

The front window of Dan's house is broken. There are muddy size-10 footprints leading from the window to the china cabinet.

All of Dan's expensive china is missing.

When you walk back to the broken window, you see a white van on the street. A man in a white hat is putting an open box of china into the back of the van.

When the man walks around to the driver's door, he leaves a trail of muddy size-10 footprints.

The van roars off.

Who stole Dan's china?

(A) The man in the white hat.
(B) Someone who really likes
    china.

Answer:

(B) Someone who really likes
china.

There would be no reason to steal
china if you did not really like china.

Also, it cannot be the man in the
white hat. He was smiling and seems
like a nice guy.

Emilio looks up from my wisdom-filled guide.

"Give me your honest assessment," I tell him.

"It doesn't make any sense," he says.

"That's a demerit," I announce.

"But you said to give you my honest assessment."

"No one who says they want your honest assessment actually wants your honest assessment. Especially if it's critical."

"Okay, but the answer says it can't be the guy in the white hat because he was smiling. Though nowhere in the scenario do you say he was smiling."

"Yes," I answer. "That part must be assumed."

"Timmy, I don't think you can—"

"Stop," I say. "You do not understand great literature." I flip through the pages. "Read this next scenario instead. It may be more suited to your reading comprehension level."

Old Man Johnson is in the study of his mansion.

The temperature outside is 88 degrees Fahrenheit.

The barometric pressure is 30.15.

The mansion is 36 feet tall.

He has three dogs, two of whom are dead.

So technically, he has one dog.

Johnson decides to read a book.

So he scans the dusty shelves until he finds the one he is looking for: *Tight Buns in Six Easy Workouts*.

But when he opens the book, he sees that all the print is upside down.

So he turns the book upside down in order to read it.

When he does so, a suspicious white powder spills from the pages of the book onto his lap.

Johnson breathes it in and is dead in three minutes.

Who killed Johnson?

(A) The author of *Tight Buns in Six Easy Workouts*.
(B) His lone remaining dog.

Answer: Unknown.

But the important part is that you learned nothing from Johnson's example. Because to read this, you turned the book upside down, thereby risking the exact same thing that happened to Johnson.

Emilio begins to speak. But I stop him.

"Let the genius wash over you," I tell him. "I am a once-in-a-generation writer."

Emilio stands in silent awe.

"Now I will bang out a few more of these scenarios on my mother's laptop," I tell him. "And when I am finished, your work will begin. Publicity. Promotional tours. The works."

"Timmy," he says, "this really doesn't sound like a good—"

"Start with a local bookstore here in Key West. Organize a signing. Promote it heavily. I'll even do the talk-show circuit if I must."

Emilio rubs his eyes.

"And work on your attitude," I tell my unpaid intern. "It's very negative. Remember: If you are determined to succeed in life, nothing can stop you. Except maybe a truck. Because if a truck runs you over, you'd pretty much be stopped."

And immediately, I visualize that as an inspirational poster.

IF YOU ARE DETERMINED TO SUCCEED IN LIFE, NOTHING CAN STOP YOU, EXCEPT MAYBE A TRUCK. BECAUSE IF A TRUCK RUNS YOU OVER, YOU'D PRETTY MUCH BE STOPPED.
— T. FAILURE

"Get ten thousand of those made," I tell him. "I want to see that poster in every bookstore in this country."

I pat him on the back for encouragement.

And at that moment, I realize that there is nothing standing between me and success.

And then I am hit by a truck.

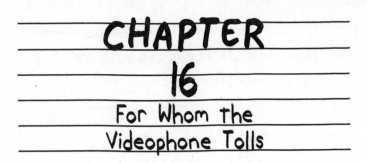

CHAPTER
16
For Whom the Videophone Tolls

"Corrina Corrina is on the phone!" my mother shouts from the other room.

I stand, mouth agape.

"Surely this is some kind of cruel hoax," I say as I enter the room. "Informing me that my mortal enemy has telephoned our vacation abode. And right in the middle of critical business."

"Shhhh," my mother says. "She's gonna hear you."

So I pick up my mother's cell phone.

"Failure, Inc.," I say into the phone. "Now with expanded operations in the Florida Keys. Dominating the detective universe as always. With whom am I speaking?"

But no one answers.

ME→   ←NO ONE

"Oh, wonderful," I tell my mother. "So it *was* a hoax. Well, I for one was not fooled. But I hope you enjoyed the unpleasantness you caused."

"What are you talking about?" asks my mother.

"Mother, Corrina Corrina is the Evil One. An unethical detective who joined the Dark

Side and brought dishonor to our craft. She is a thief. She is unpleasant. She is rude. She is deceitful. She is ruthless. She is corrupt."

"Timmy—" my mom interrupts.

"I'm not finished, Mother," I answer before continuing. "She is pathetic. She is egotistical. She is underhand. She is psychotic. She is a fraud. And she has tried many times to destroy my detective business. And if that's not enough, I do not approve of her saucy hairstyle."

CORRINA CORRINA → ← SAUCY HAIRSTYLE

"Timmy, Corrina Corrina is not on the cell phone. She's on the videophone. *On the laptop right in front of you.*"

I look at the kitchen table. And there, for all to see, is the Evil One.

Spying.

"Hi, Timmy," says Corrina Corrina, waving from the computer screen.

"ARRRRGGGGGHHHH," I scream. *"How did she get in our house?!"*

But my mother is no help.

So I lunge for a jumbo box of Mr. Froggie Flaky Flakes.

"What are you doing, Timmy?" asks my mother.

And ignoring her, I pour the Mr. Froggie Flaky Flakes all over the floor.

"Timmy!" yells my mother. *What in the world do you—?*"

But before she can finish her question, I thrust the now-empty box of Mr. Froggie Flaky Flakes over the laptop's screen.

"There!" I announce triumphantly. "Now she will no longer be able to canvas our house for valuables."

"Timmy," my mother interrupts, "when you are done with your phone call, you are going to pick up every single piece of this cereal, and then you and I are going to have a little talk."

"Fine," I answer. "Mistakes were made. Though I blame you for the security breach. And I should probably get credit for saving your valuables from impending thievery."

My mother walks outside, slamming the door to the verandah.

"I think your screen cut out," says Corrina Corrina.

"It did not 'cut out,'" I inform the Damsel of Darkness. "I have outwitted you. Now speak your piece. For you will get no valuables from this abode."

"Okay, well," she stumbles along, "Mr. Jenkins has picked me to be his teacher's assistant for summer school and—"

"Oh, good God," I interject. "This has debacle written all over it."

"And as teacher's assistant," she continues, "I have to make sure that each student picks a history book to do a book report on."

"Fine," I answer, eager to get her off the videophone. "Give me the shortest book. Perhaps the length of a bumper sticker."

AND THEY LIVED HAPPILY EVER AFTER. THE END.

"Well, the shortest book is Thomas Paine's *Common Sense*. But Nunzio Benedici chose it. And we can't have two students doing the same book."

"Fine, give me the next shortest book. And hurry. I do not have time for this trivial conversation."

"Well, you see, that's sort of the bad news," says the Mistress of Mendacity. "All the short books are taken. In fact, *all* of the books are taken. Except one. Shelby Foote's Civil War trilogy."

"Good," I answer. "I'll take it. Is it pamphlet size?"

She takes a moment before she answers.

"It's three thousand pages."

CHAPTER
17
Yo Ho Ho and a Bottle of Rumination

Dear Total,

I am shipping ye three large books.

Ye are to do a book report.

This is ye chance to redeem ye-self.

For as ye know, ye have betrayed ye former business partner.

I can only hope that ye actions have caused ye a great deal of guilt.

And that ye are suffering suitably for ye sins.

CHAPTER 18
Meet the Failures

If you ever become a famous author and want to kick off a book tour in Key West, Florida, do not hire Emilio Empanada to be your promotional manager.

For if you do, the massive, stadium-size crowds you are expecting will look like this:

(THIS SPACE INTENTIONALLY LEFT BLANK.)

That's right. There is nothing there.

Because there is nobody at this book signing.

"You have embarrassed me profoundly," I inform Emilio Empanada. "I should never have put you in charge of promotion."

"Wait," says Emilio. "Here comes somebody."

It is true. Our first customer. The first of perhaps millions.

"Hello, sir," I say, holding out my hand. "I suppose you would like to shake the hand of Timmy Failure, author of *Timmy Failure's Wisdom-Filled Guide for the Uneducated People Who Don't Know Very Much.*"

Meet
TIMMY FAILURE

"Actually, I was just wondering—do you fellas know if this place has a bathroom?"

"To the left at the back," says Emilio Empanada, much too cheerily.

"Oh, good," I tell Emilio as the man walks off. "You can direct people to the bathroom. Perhaps that could be your next job after I fire you as my promotional manager."

RIGHT THIS WAY, FOLKS.

BATHROOM DIRECTIONAL COORDINATOR

"Timmy, the promotional stuff was hard," says Emilio Empanada. "Nobody would even let us use their bookstore."

"Yes, well, what do you call where we are now?" I answer.

"The sidewalk *in front* of a bookstore," he says. "Until they catch us."

"A bookstore is a bookstore," I remind him. "And you're lucky I found this place."

"Yes, but we are here without permission," says Emilio. "On a card table we found at our rental house."

"You need to worry less about the law and more about why you did not promote this event properly."

"What did you want me to do?"

"Inspire people!" I shout at my promotional manager. "Like this."

IF YOU ARE DETERMINED TO SUCCEED IN LIFE, NOTHING CAN STOP YOU. EXCEPT MAYBE A TRUCK. BECAUSE IF A TRUCK RUNS YOU OVER, YOU'D PRETTY MUCH BE STOPPED.

—T. F.

Meet
TIMMY FAILURE

"Timmy, you cannot put that sign up over the store's window."

But he is wrong. For I immediately inspire people.

"What are you boys selling?" asks an old woman.

"Timmy Failure's Wisdom-Filled Guide for the Uneducated People Who Don't Know Very Much," Emilio answers. "Ten dollars per copy. A hundred if you want the author here to sign it."

"And three hundred if you'd like me to pose for a photo with you," I add.

"And is that why you have that table out here?" asks the old woman.

"Yes," I answer. "To sell books to the many fans like yourself."

She smiles as she opens her wallet.
And we immediately make a sale.

CHAPTER 19

Whimsical Graffiti

"I can't believe you sold her the card table," says Emilio Empanada.

"I didn't sell her the card table, Emilio," I answer. "I sold her five copies of my book for fifty dollars. The table was a bonus gift."

"Yeah, but she said she would just recycle the books."

"Of course she said that. She's old. What she meant to say was 'cherish.'"

"Still," says Emilio. "You're giving away parts of the rental house."

"Will you please keep your voice down?" I whisper to Emilio. "My mother is sitting right in front of you. And this journey is painful enough already."

And it's true.

For we are touring the island on the painfully slow Tooty Toot Train.

And at the very moment Emilio and I should be using our newfound wealth to climb to the top of the lighthouse and find my would-be assailant, we are being paraded through the town at a paltry two miles per hour.

"Can't this thing go any faster?" I yell to the driver. "I'm like a sitting duck back here."

"Timmy!" my mother says, glaring back at me. "Enough."

"And to our left," says the train driver, "we have a museum dedicated to all the many shipwreck treasures found off the coast of Key West through the years, the most famous being in 1985, when the wreck of a Spanish galleon was found, yielding an estimated four hundred million dollars in gold and silver."

"Ooooh," says Emilio. "That's incredible."

"It's hardly incredible," I tell Emilio. "It's boring. All history is boring."

And as I say it, I think of my summer school history class.

And how hard my polar bear must be working at this very moment to complete my book report.

Mercifully, the Tooty Toot Train finally stops near a palm-tree-shrouded restaurant with a large brick courtyard. Everyone gets off.

"Good, it's over," I announce, hopping off. "Now me and Emilio have to go."

"Nope," says Dave, guiding me toward the restaurant. "You're gonna come in here and eat dinner with us."

I turn to my mother. "Does he get to tell me that?"

"Yes," she says, always taking the wrong side in these disputes.

"Well, that's odd," I tell her. "Because it really feels like your boyfriend is impinging on my personal freedoms."

"Husband," she says.

"So you allege," I answer. "I think the important point here is for us to give Dave some personal boundaries. You know, like how he doesn't get to tell me what to do."

My mother drags me through the courtyard to one of the outdoor tables.

"You will sit down and you will eat," she says. "You're embarrassing yourself in front of Emilio."

Emilio says nothing.

"I really should have fled to Cuba," I mutter. "I understand they have more personal freedom there."

"What did you just say?" asks my mother.

Anxiety-ridden, Emilio begins rearranging his silverware. "The salad fork should always go on the *outside* of the dinner fork," he announces.

"Tell me what you just said," my mother says to me, her voice rising.

"And the dinner fork," continues Emilio, "always goes to the right of the plate."

"Emilio," says Dave. "Enough with the forks."

"Then may I please be excused to use the

bathroom?" says Emilio. "I really need to wash my hands."

Dave nods.

"I need to use the bathroom, too," I add.

"After you tell your mother what you said," says Dave.

I stare at him.

"I didn't say anything, Dave."

The restaurant feels suddenly quiet.

"Now may I please use the bathroom?" I ask. "We were on that train forever."

Dave stares at my mother. My mother says nothing.

"Go," says Dave.

So I walk through the courtyard to the bathroom.

And when I get there, I see Emilio coming out of the women's room.

"The men's room was occupied," says Emilio. "I didn't think anyone would mind."

But the men's room is now free.

And so I go inside.

And see a wall of graffiti on the stall door. Each etching more nonsensical than the last.

Until I spot one item in the center of the door.

That is all too sensical.

TIMMY FAILURE
IS NO SAILOR.
NOW HE'S SCARED,
HIS FACE IS PALER.

CHAPTER
20
Sharp at First Light

"How dare he mock my nautical skills," I tell Emilio Empanada as he lies on his bed reading *The Donkey's Kiss Is More Powerful Than His Kick*.

"It's malicious," says Emilio.

"And I look nothing like that," I add.

"You don't," he answers.

"The important thing now is to not get rattled," I tell my unpaid intern. "Because that's what my nemesis wants."

"Yes," says Emilio. "I imagine that's what he or she wants. So what do we do next?"

"Well, if the stupid lighthouse hadn't been

closed, we would have rushed there. But that will have to wait until morning."

"And until then?" asks Emilio.

"We keep the doors locked and our detective minds sharp," I tell him. "Tomorrow is the biggest day of our lives."

"I'll keep sharp by reading this romance novel," says Emilio. "*The Donkey's Kiss* is quite intellectually stimulating."

"And I'll keep sharp by adding a few chapters to my bestseller," I tell him. "The public's demand for these books appears to be insatiable."

Emilio says nothing.

"In fact, I've already written a new scenario inspired by the events of tonight. It's both instructive and riveting."

"Oh," replies Emilio.

"You may once again read it without charge," I tell him. "Though tips would be welcome."

He puts his romance novel down and reads.

A prominent detective is dining in a Key West establishment.

Suddenly, a man in a white hat rushes out of the men's room carrying a black Sharpie pen.

The back of his shirt says "Key West Penmanship Champ, 2012–2016."

When he sees the detective, he freezes.

"I didn't write that on the stall door," he says to the detective. "I swear. I didn't write anything." He drops the pen and runs.

The detective enters the men's room.

On the stall door, he sees a threat against his life.

It is written in black Sharpie.

The penmanship is exquisite.

In the corner of the bathroom is a security camera.

When the restaurant allows the

detective to view the videotape, he sees the man in the white hat writing on the stall door.

Who threatened the detective?

(A) The man in the white hat.
(B) Capuchin monkeys.

Answer: None of the above.

The man in the white hat said he didn't write it. So it can't be him.

Neither can it be a capuchin monkey. Their penmanship is poor.

This mystery will have to go unsolved.

"Couldn't the man have just lied?" asks Emilio Empanada.

"No," I answer. "Not a man in a white hat."

"Why not?" he asks.

"Oh, my goodness," I answer, rather stunned. "I had no idea you were such a novice. Haven't you ever seen a western? You know, with good guys and bad guys?"

"I guess," says Emilio.

"Then you know the good guy always wears a white hat."

BAD GUY   GOOD GUY

"Oh," he answers.

I turn off his bedside lamp.

"What are you doing?" he asks.

"You're not sharp," I tell him. "You need sleep. We can't have you with this impaired judgment tomorrow."

"Okay," he says. "Good night."

"Good night, unpaid intern."

CHAPTER
21
True at First Lighthouse

We are up at dawn and on our way to the lighthouse.

Menaced by more chickens.

"Look what you've done," I tell Emilio Empanada.

"What's wrong with chickens?"

"They could be spies."

"I think they're just chickens," says Emilio.

"Anything with two eyes and a mouth can be a spy," I explain to my unpaid intern.

"I didn't know that."

"There's a lot you don't know," I say, stopping suddenly on the sidewalk. "Like why is there a long line of people waiting for the lighthouse at nine thirty in the morning?"

"I don't think these people are going to the lighthouse," says Emilio. "I think they're going to that big house across the street."

He points to a two-storey house with lime-green shutters.

"Whose house is that?"

"Some famous author."

"Oh, goodness. I can think of nothing more boring than talking to an author."

"I think he's dead," replies Emilio.

"Well, now that could be interesting. Does he say much?"

"No, he's not there. He's dead."

"Well, then let's hurry and get in line for the lighthouse before they figure that out."

So we walk up to the lighthouse.

But there is no line.

And no Lighthouse Larry.

"Who are you?" I ask the boy beating on bongos.

"Billy," he says. "Who are you?"

"We're two guests who wish to enter your lighthouse," I answer. "We have the necessary funds."

"It's not my lighthouse," he says. "I'm just sitting here till my dad gets back with our conch fritters."

"Larry," I say.

"You know my dad?"

"Unfortunately, yes," I answer. "We are in the midst of bitter, protracted litigation."

"I don't know what that means."

"It means I was mauled by one of your attack chickens."

Billy laughs.

"That's very callous of you, Billy. Please just take our money so we can get on with our business. I'm a detective and this is my unpaid intern," I say, pointing to Emilio. "And we have no time for your mirth-filled mockery."

"Detective?" says Billy. "Like cops and robbers? Can I play?"

Before I can react, I am struck in the face by a thick jet of water.

"Oh, good God!" I cry, falling to the ground.

"It's just a squirt gun," says Bongo Billy.

"I'm dying," I answer.

"You're fine," offers my unpaid intern.

"I regret that I have but one life to give for my detective business," I announce as I breathe my last.

"You're kind of weird," says Bongo Billy, banging once again on his bongos.

"Play Chopin's *Funeral March* if you know it," I gasp. "It's my final request. Though I'm not sure it's particularly suited for the bongo."

"Here," says Bongo Billy, handing me a plump pink water balloon. "You can hit me with this. Then we'll be even."

"Absurd," I announce, miraculously cured by an act of providence. "Then you will sue me, as I am suing your father."

I rise like Lazarus brought forth from the grave.

"But I will accept your plump pink water balloon in the spirit of compromise with which it is offered."

I cradle the balloon like it is a newborn chicken.

And Emilio cradles a newborn chicken like it is a newborn chicken.

And we storm our tower of destiny.

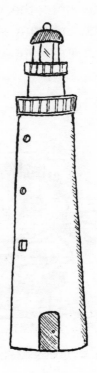

CHAPTER
22
Down the Up Staircase

I race up the eighty-eight stairs of the spiral staircase until I reach the top of the lighthouse. And leaping out onto the observation deck, I see *everything* on this frontier island of doom.

Like the blue sea and the cruise ships.
And the steeples and the palm trees.
And the white roofs and the people.
Each more suspicious than the last.

Like the man in the Speedos.

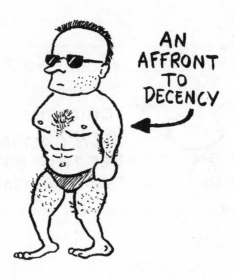

And the baby on the head.

And the chicken on the chickens.

TOWER OF
CHICKENS
(DIDN'T ACTUALLY
SEE THIS, BUT
COULD PROBABLY
HAPPEN.)

And as I quickly scan the frond-shrouded streets to find our rental house, I am confident that from here I will spot my nemesis. Running. Crouching. Hiding.

Screaming.

There is someone screaming.

"TIIIIIIIIIIIIIIIIIIIIIIIIIIIMMMMMMMMM-MMY!"

I pop my head back inside the lighthouse. "Emilio?"

"YES!" His voice echoes up from the curved white walls. "I've been yelling forever. I'm stuck!"

"Stuck how?"

"Halfway up the staircase. I can't move."

"What do you mean you can't move? Are your legs broken or something?"

"No, my legs aren't broken. I just started running up the stairs and then I looked down and now I can't move."

"You're *scared*? At the most pivotal moment of our investigation, you're *scared*?"

"Maybe," he says, his voice echoing through the lighthouse. "Okay, more than maybe."

"Well, just grab the railing and move up here slowly. I'm on the trail of a killer!"

"I can't!" he yells. "I'm with Edward Higglebottom the Third."

"Who the heck is that?"

"My baby chicken. I just named him. And I need both my hands to hold him."

"Who brings a baby chicken to a criminal pursuit?" I cry out. "It's very unprofessional!"

"I just found him walking around outside. He was all by himself. No mother or father or anything. Please, Timmy. I just need your help going back down the stairs."

"Emilio Empanada! I am in the most strategically advantageous spot on this entire island and I am holding a plump pink water balloon. If I can just get two uninterrupted minutes, I will find my nemesis and stun him with this watery projectile."

I hear nothing in reply, so I leap back onto the observation deck and raise my plump pink water balloon high overhead and search for assassins.

And as I do, a rumbling echo rises back up the lighthouse.

"TIIIIIIIIIIIIIIIIIIIIIIIIIMMMMMMM-MMY!"

"Oh, good gosh," I mutter, "I give up." I lay the plump pink water balloon on the observation deck, then hop back inside and descend the staircase.

And save Emilio Empanada from himself.

CHAPTER 23

Yes, His Name Was Steve and When He Walked Me Home Da Doo Ron Ron Ron Da Doo Ron Ron

On the way back from the lighthouse, we are once again escorted.

Though this time not by chickens.

"Is this your son?" asks the man who has walked us home.

"Yes," says my mother, poking her head out the front door. "Is something wrong?"

"He pelted me with a water balloon from the top of the Key West lighthouse."

My mother looks at me.

"I placed the balloon on the observation deck," I explain. "It then rolled off and struck Speedo Steve."

"My name is Ron, not Steve," says Speedo Steve. "And I find it hard to believe it was an accident."

"And why is that?" asks my mother. "If I may ask."

"Because the whole way home, your son

was saying, 'Ye got what ye deserve, ye Speedo-wearing fiend.'"

"I deny that," I tell my mother. "I do not talk like a pirate."

"He was talking like a pirate," says Speedo Steve.

"His memory of events is compromised," I tell my mother. "For by his own admission, he was struck in the head by a water balloon. My guess is that he is drifting in and out of consciousness. He doesn't even know his name."

"My name is Ron," says Speedo Steve.

"Timmy, did you hit this man with a water balloon on purpose?" asks my mother.

"Preposterous," I say, shaking my head.

She turns to Emilio.

"Emilio, did Timmy do it on purpose?"

"Avast!" I object. "You would take the word of an unpaid intern over that of your son?"

"Emilio, did he do it on purpose?" she repeats.

"I wouldn't know," answers Emilio. "Honest. I was stuck in the lighthouse, holding Edward Higglebottom the Third."

"Who?" asks my confused mother.

He holds up his baby chicken.

Edward Higglebottom the Third

"That settles it," I tell my mother. "There are no witnesses and thus it is the word of your beloved son, Timmy, versus that of the unseemly Speedo Steve."

"Ron," he says. "For the last time, *Ron*."

"And before you believe a word that he says," I add, "consider how the man is dressed. It is an affront to good taste and decency."

"Okay, Timmy, that's enough," says my mother.

"A crime of fashion," I add.

CRIME
OF
FASHION

"Sir, whatever happened," says my mother, "it will never happen again. I assure you."

"Well, thank you," he says before pausing. "And I'm sorry. I didn't catch your name."

"Patty," says my mom.

"Well, thank you, Patty," he says, shaking my mom's hand.

"And thank *you*, Steve," she answers.

"Ron," he says from behind clenched teeth. *"My name is Ron."*

CHAPTER 24
Unforgivable, That's What You Are

"What is wrong with you lately?" asks my mother. "First throwing cereal all over the floor. Then being rude at dinner. Now tossing water balloons."

"I deny everything," I answer.

"And what's this about a book report that's due?" she adds. "I got an e-mail from Corrina Corrina."

"An e-mail?!" I exclaim. "Did you open it?"

"Yes, I opened it."

"Oh, good gosh," I exclaim, slapping my forehead. "Mother, this is Corrina Corrina we are talking about. Her e-mail was no doubt infected by a computer virus. I'm sure that by now your laptop has spontaneously combusted."

SPONTANEOUSLY COMBUSTED LAPTOP

"Or is somehow hatching evil spiders," I add.

EVIL SPIDERS

"My laptop is fine, Timmy. Now tell me about this book report. Is there a book I need to buy you?"

"No, Mother. It is all under control."

"You promise?"

"Yes," I answer. "Now I may go? I think

I heard a knock on the door."

"Funny," she answers. "I didn't hear anything."

"Well, I did. Perhaps it's your new best friend, Speedo Steve, no doubt back to spread malicious falsehoods."

And so I open the front door.

And find a telegram lying on the doorstep.

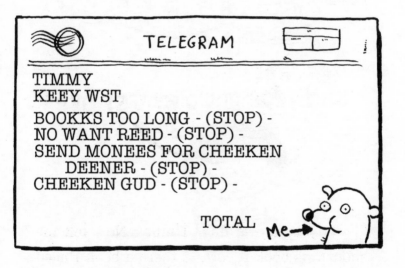

TELEGRAM

TIMMY
KEEY WST

BOOKKS TOO LONG - (STOP) -
NO WANT REED - (STOP) -
SEND MONEES FOR CHEEKEN
    DEENER - (STOP) -
CHEEKEN GUD - (STOP) -

TOTAL   Me→

It is a profound blow.

And one that immediately threatens my academic future.

So I think fast.

And instantly hatch a Plan B.

An elaborate step-by-step scheme that involves the following:

STEP ONE: EMILIO READS

STEP TWO: EMILIO WRITES MY BOOK REPORT

So I burst into the bedroom and find my unpaid intern.

"You have done something unforgivable," I announce to Emilio Empanada.

"What'd I do?" he asks, looking up wide-eyed from the cardboard box that now holds Edward Higglebottom the Third.

"You have shown fear during a mission," I announce. "It is the one unforgivable sin of detective life."

"So what now?"

"I forgive you."

"I thought it was unforgivable."

"Don't confuse yourself with the details," I explain. "The point is that your forgiveness is conditional on whether or not you can do something for me."

"What is it?" he asks.

"It cannot be discussed here. For my

nemesis has shown the ability to penetrate this very room. As such, he could hop out at any moment and kill us both."

Emilio gasps.

"Also, my mother is in the next room. And if she hears me, I could be grounded."

Emilio gasps again.

"Meet me at global headquarters in one hour," I whisper.

And leaping out of the window, I slide down the balcony support and race toward the sea.

CHAPTER
25
Pier Review

I pace the dock of Failure, Inc.'s Temporary Global Headquarters, waiting for the arrival of my unpaid intern.

And as I pace, I stare out at the sea, hoping for a glimpse of Cuba and the fat bear who has betrayed me.

Fearful of the unprofessional behavior I might see.

"I hope that you get no money!" I yell from the end of the dock. "And no chicken!"

I shake my fist toward the sea.

"Ohh, the guilt you must feel!" I add.

But all I hear in response is the gentle lapping of the waves upon the pier.

And a voice.

"I don't feel any guilt."

I wheel around.

And there, in the Top-Secret, Heavily-Guarded, No-One-Can-Ever-Know, Super-Hidden, Hyper-Vigilant, All-But-Impenetrable Temporary Global Headquarters of Failure, Inc . . .

Is my mother.

"What are *you* doing here?!" I cry.

"I came to talk to you," she says.

"Oh, great. So Emilio Empanada told you all about my plans for the book report and now I'm dead."

"What plans for the book report?"

I pause.

"You must have misheard me," I answer. "I said 'beak report.' I'm having Emilio count all the bird beaks on this island. The boy loves his chickens."

ONE...TWO...THREE...

"I don't know what you're talking about," says my mom. "But that's not why I'm here."

"Well, you obviously talked to him," I answer. "Who else would tell you where the Super-Hidden Global Headquarters was located?"

"I can see you from the house, Timmy. In fact, every house on our block has a view of this pier."

I make a note in my detective log.

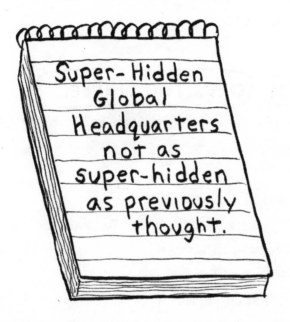

Super-Hidden Global Headquarters not as super-hidden as previously thought.

"Fine. So you're a spy," I tell my mother.

"No," she says. "But that is sort of related to why I'm here."

"Aha!" I cry. "You *used* to be a spy and now you're swimming to Cuba and fleeing."

MOTHER
(TRAITOR TO HER
COUNTRY)

"No," she says.

"It's farther than it looks," I warn her. "But best of luck. And thank you for raising me."

She shakes her head.

"Timmy, Emilio is the person who's been writing you those notes."

I stare at her.

"That can't be."

"It is," she says. "But don't blame him. Blame me. I was telling Dave how bored you were down here without your detective work and Dave was saying that it would be fun to give you a detective case that could be sort of a game that you could play and—"

"It's not a game, Mother," I interrupt her. *"My profession is not a game."*

"I know, I know," she says, brushing the hair from my eyes. "But the point is, I think Emilio overheard us and just decided to do it himself."

"But that can't be. There was a note that just fell out of a random book."

"*His* book," she says. "He put it there."

"But there was the graffiti in the men's room," I continue. "He didn't even use the men's room."

"Yes, he did," says my mother. "Right before you got there. Then he walked out of the women's room to throw you off."

"Balderdash!" I cry. "I am a trained detective. I am aware of my surroundings at all times."

"Well, if you recall, that was a rather tense moment at the table. Maybe you let your guard slip for a second."

"My guard never slips," I remind her. "Emilio's obviously lying. How do you even know all this?"

"Emilio talked to me. Right after you left for the pier. I think he just felt guilty for letting it get this far and he didn't know what to do, so he came to me."

I quietly pace the dock.

"I promise that nobody meant you any harm," she says as I watch the waves. "Not me. Not Dave. And especially not Emilio."

I watch as a pair of dark-black cormorants dive from the sky and into the shallow green waters.

"Do you understand?" she asks.

I pause before answering.

"I do," I answer.

"I'm glad," she says.

And I wheel around to face her.

"Emilio Empanada is a double agent."

CHAPTER 26

Rinsing Your Mouth Out with Soaps

U.S. Route 1 begins in the remote town of Fort Kent, Maine, and meanders 2,369 long miles through fourteen different states until it finally finds its way to the balmy coral island that is Key West, Florida.

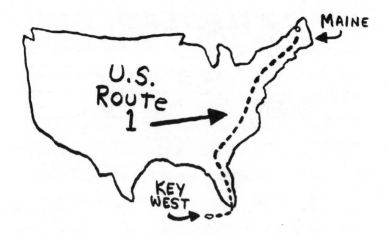

There, the longest north-south highway in the United States comes to a dead stop.

The literal end of the road.

And so, if you are villainous or treacherous and escaping the law via the country's highways, Key West is the farthest south your tired car can go.

And as such, like a pool filter catching fallen leaves, Key West snares more than its fair share of international criminals and spies.

None more prominent than the one I have tied up in my bedroom.

"Who are you working for?" I ask the suspect.

"Nobody," says Emilio.

"Who put you up to this?" I ask.

"Nobody," says Emilio.

"Who told you to write those notes?" I ask.

"Nobody," says Emilio. "Timmy, I did it all myself. I'm not working for anybody."

"I'm sorry to hear that, Emilio Empanada. Because if you're not going to answer my questions, you leave me no choice but to get rough."

I turn on the television in front of him.

"What are you doing?" asks Emilio.

"Putting on daytime soap operas," I answer. "It is the worst torture a human being can endure."

I look to see if he flinches. Remarkably, he does not.

"The first show will be *Days of Our Miserable Lives*. When it concludes, you will watch *The Misguided Light*, and then another and another and another, until you decide to get smart and talk."

"Okay," he says.

"This could get ugly," I warn him.

"It's fine," he answers. "I'll just sit here and watch soaps."

So I pause to make a note in my detective log.

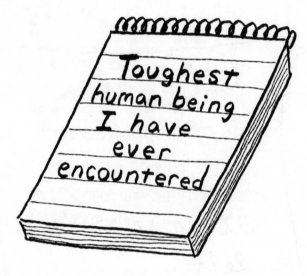

CHAPTER
27
Writing a Plank Cheque

I use Emilio's soap opera time to write a reply to my wayward polar bear.

Dear Total,

I am sending ye $40.

It is all I have left.

Now write the book report.

Or I shall come to
Cuba and make ye
walk the plank.
CREEEEAK
Yours at Sea,
Pirate Jimmy

CHAPTER
28
Shell of Himself

I return to the interrogation room, bracing myself for the tortured squalor that the subject will be living in after three uninterrupted hours of watching soap operas.

"Ready to talk?" I say in a steely-cold voice as I kick open the door.

"I sure am!" he answers.

"Jennifer is going to have John's baby!" he beams. *"And John's not even her husband!"*

I am stunned into silence.

"And Kelly and Dave—they're getting divorced. I thought they could make it, but not now. *She shot him with a harpoon!*"

He swivels his head back toward the television.

"That woman on the screen now is Anna. She's a LIAR LIAR PANTS ON FIRE! But she may have drowned when she fell off Scott's boat. And if so, *good riddance!*"

"You were not supposed to *enjoy* the soap operas, Emilio Empanada!"

"Sorry," he says. "But they're so scandalous! Now untie me so I can feed my chicken."

"Fine," I say, untying him. "But if you're not gonna talk, then it's no more soap operas for you!"

"Timmy," he says as he feeds Edward Higglebottom the Third, "there's nothing more to say. *I* wrote the notes. *Me*. Nobody else. There is no criminal. No nemesis. No enemy to find."

I sit on his bed and watch as he feeds his baby chicken.

"And I'm sorry," he continues. "Really sorry. I just did it because you didn't seem happy here and I thought having a mystery to solve would be fun. But that's it. Whether you let me watch soap operas or not, there's nothing else to say. No secrets to tell. Nothing."

He holds out his baby chicken.

"Want to hold him?"

"No," I answer. "They attack."

And as I say it, there is a loud *CRACK* against the bedroom window, followed by a heavy *THUD* upon the verandah.

So we rush to the window and look down.

And see a conch shell.

The kind you use to hear the soothing sound of the ocean.

But there is nothing soothing coming from this shell.

There is only a note.

CHAPTER
29
Last Train to Treasureville

We rush to the only captain I know—the seaman who trusted me with his boat.

"Maybe we should tell your mom or Uncle Dave about the conch note," says Emilio Empanada as we run along the beach to the wharf. "Because I didn't write this one, Timmy! And this could be dangerous."

"You're with a trained detective," I tell Emilio. "So there's nothing to worry about. Plus, if anything goes wrong, I have the Fists of Fury."

FISTS OF FURY

"Do you even know where this captain friend of yours keeps his boat?" asks Emilio.

"Well, we took off from the big harbor on the north side of the island."

Emilio stops running. "That's miles from here, Timmy. We need to take a taxi or something."

"Are you kidding? We don't have money for a taxi."

"Don't we still have forty dollars left from selling the table?"

"From *selling the books*, you mean. But no. It went to my former business partner. He's currently blackmailing me to get free chicken. It's an ugly international affair, and I'd rather not get you involved."

"Well, fine, but we can't walk to the port. It's hot. And *humid*. And I don't want my shirt to get perspiration stains."

"Oh, fine," I say, giving up. "We have one other option."

"What is it?" asks Emilio.

"This is wonderful!" says Emilio. "I can't believe our ticket stubs let us ride for the full week."

"It's not wonderful. It's humiliating. Plus we have to listen to the train driver say the same stupid things all over again."

"And to our left," says the driver, "we have a museum dedicated to all the many shipwreck treasures found off the coast of Key West through the years, the most famous being in 1985, when the wreck of a Spanish galleon was found, yielding an estimated four hundred million dollars in gold and—"

"Did he say treasure?" I ask Emilio.

"Yes," answers Emilio. "I tried to tell you how incredible it was when we heard it the last time. But you said it was boring."

"Yes, because last time he didn't say anything about treasure."

"Yes, he did," says Emilio.

"No, he didn't," I reply.

"Yes, he did."

"No, he didn't."[1]

"Fine. I don't want to argue," says Emilio. "It's interesting either way."

"It's more than interesting," I answer, cool as a sea cucumber. "It's the answer to our mystery."

---

1. He did not. You can go back to that chapter and check. And if he did, that is only because someone has altered your book to make me look bad. Shame on whoever doctored your book.

CHAPTER
30
A Farewell to Farms

"Captain Largo Spargo is a grizzled, salty sailor of the sea," I tell Emilio Empanada as the bright-pink Tooty Toot Train lets us off at the harbor. "He's been shipwrecked, shot, capsized, and captured. And he's given as good as he's got, once stabbing over six dozen mutineers. And don't stare, but I think he has a wooden leg."

"Whoa," says Emilio, no doubt imagining the heavily scarred captain.

"I should add that he drinks rum by the barrel, smokes tobacco by the bale, and has a temper so bad that he'd rather kill a man than correct him. So whatever you do, watch what you say or you could be shark chum."

SHARK CHUM

"Oh, my goodness," says Emilio. "Then I'll let *you* do the talking."

Which is wise.

Because as soon as we get to the dock, the captain is running toward us.

"Hey, you're that little kid who was vomiting all day," says Captain Largo Spargo.

"I was your co-captain on the voyage," I correct him. "But yes, it is I. And this time I'm here on business."

"Who's your friend?" he asks, wiping his brow with a small towel.

"My unpaid intern," I answer.

Emilio just stares. "*You're* Captain Largo Spargo?" he asks.

"I don't know who that is," says the captain. "But my name is Bruce."

"'Bruce' on land," I whisper to Emilio. "'Largo Spargo' at sea. Sailors have many aliases."

"Well, you look nothing like I expected," says Emilio.

"Yeah? Well, you caught me jogging today. I've been doing it three times a week. Really helps keep the old ticker strong. Plus, my cholesterol is terrific."

"Let me cut right to the chase," I respectfully interject, not wishing to anger him.

"Okay, but do you mind following me to that food cart across the street while you talk?" says the grizzled sea captain. "I want to get a bran muffin and some Greek yogurt."

So we follow him to get a bran muffin.

"Captain, my life has been threatened," I explain as we walk. "By somebody who wants me to stay away from the money. A *captain's* money."

"Wow. Well, it's sure not my money," he says, taking a bite from his bran muffin. "I mean, I used to have money, back when I was an organic farmer in Connecticut. But last year I said good-bye to all that and put my savings into this charter fishing boat here in—"

"So which one is fake?" interrupts Emilio, staring at the captain's legs. "The peg leg, I mean. Which one is it?"

"Peg leg?" answers the captain, glancing down at his sweaty thighs. "What are you talking about?"

"Well, Timmy was saying—"

"Never mind what I was saying!" I admonish my intern. "The captain here doesn't have time for your landlubber buffoonery. Are you *trying* to irritate him?"

"Oh, God," says Emilio, clasping his hands together. "Please don't make me shark chum."

"Shark chum?" says the captain. "Listen, I don't want to hurry you two, but if you have something to say, you might want to say it quickly. I'm attending a poetry reading at Key West Books in about fifteen minutes and I still have to shower."

"I know that store well," I tell the ancient mariner. "I did a very successful book signing there."

"On the sidewalk," adds Emilio. "We were trespassing. And we didn't sell books. We sold a table. A table we didn't own."

"DEMERIT!" I yell at my unpaid intern.

"Listen, kids, I gotta go," says the captain as Emilio makes an X in his notebook. "Maybe we can talk some other time."

"Wait!" I say as he recedes down the pier.

"What?" he asks, turning around.

"Captain, there is treasure somewhere around this island," I say, cool as a red snapper on ice. "It is large. Large enough to be worth threatening the life of a detective. And it belongs to a captain. A member of your noble profession who threatens to bring dishonor upon you all. Take me to that treasure, and I shall give you half."

The captain swallows a spoonful of yogurt and dabs the corners of his mouth with a tiny napkin.

"Listen, kids, I own a charter fishing boat," he says. "If you want to go fishing on that boat, it's two hundred a person. If you don't, that's fine, too. Either way, I have a poetry reading to attend. And I'd like to smell fresh and clean."

He throws his yogurt cup into the recycling bin.

"Always recycle," he adds.

Emilio watches him jog off and turns back toward me.

"I'm so glad he didn't stab us."

CHAPTER
31
A Clean, Well-Lighted Sidewalk

We must raise four hundred dollars to go on Largo Spargo's fishing boat.

And fast.

So I print fifty more copies of my bestseller, *Timmy Failure's Wisdom-Filled Guide for the Uneducated People Who Don't Know Very Much*, now updated with bonus material:

There is a dead man on the sidewalk.

He is bald.

The bald dead man has fallen from a seventh-storey window.

When you get to the crime scene, you look up at the window.

There, attempting to hide behind the curtains, is a man in a white hat.

He is holding a sign that says "I pushed the bald guy out the window. It was me. I did it."

Who killed the bald man?

(A) The man in the white hat.
(B) A prize pig at the county fair.

"You can't have the answer be someone who wasn't mentioned in the answers," says Emilio.

"Emilio, the public understands my genius, even if you do not. So do not attempt to edit or modify my work. For genius like this cannot be corralled. It is like a runaway donkey."

My genius

"Yes, well, your donkey has not sold a single book and we've been sitting in front of this bookstore for thirty minutes and I just know they are gonna come outside and arrest us both for trespassing."

"You are very excitable," I tell him. "It's a profound character flaw. Perhaps you should try yoga."

WHAT THAT MIGHT LOOK LIKE →

"And I'm sorry," Emilio adds, "but why'd you have to bring those lamps? There's not even a place to plug them in."

"Because they lend an air of dignity to our retail establishment," I reply. "You should know that as my promotional manager."

It is a stinging rebuke.

But a fair one.

For a few minutes later, we have our first customer.

And another successful book signing.

CHAPTER 32

Taylor Made for Timmy

"Honey, I'm trying to read, but I can't," says Doorman Dave from the bedroom next to mine. "Isn't there a light in this room?"

"Yes, the one on your nightstand," replies my mother from the kitchen.

"Yeah, well, I'm not blind," says Doorman Dave. "It's not there."

"It was there yesterday," says my mother.

"Oh, good gosh," I cry out, stomping into the hallway. "How do you expect a world-class detective to concentrate with all this mundane chatter? Emilio and I are in the midst of a critical investigation."

"Then go somewhere else and do it," says Doorman Dave from the bedroom. "This is my honeymoon. I'm allowed to talk."

I walk into the kitchen and stare at my mother.

"Look what you've wrought," I tell her.

"Go outside and play," she tells me. "You two have been cooped up in there for too long anyway."

"I do not play—I work," I remind her. "Must you disturb *and* insult me?"

"Then go outside and work," she answers.

Which is easy for her to say.

For she is not the one whose Super-Hidden Global Headquarters has been compromised.

THIS INCIDENT

So Emilio and I leave the house and sneak carefully through the dusk-lit alleys of Key West until we reach the most heavily fortified spot on the island.

"What is this?" asks Emilio.

"Fort Taylor," I answer. "An old military fort. And shockingly, no longer in use. So I hereby commandeer it for police use."

"I'm not sure we can do that," says Emilio. "I think it's against the law."

"We are the law," I remind my timid fortmate. "And the best part is that no one can sneak up on us here."

"Why is that?" asks Emilio.

"Big Bertha," I answer.

"We cannot fire a cannon at Key West vacationers," says Emilio.

"Of course not," I say. "So we start with a warning shot."

"Can we go home now?" asks Emilio. "It's getting dark."

"Not until we figure out who's writing us those notes. I have a long list of suspects."

"Well, I hope I'm not on it."

"You're not," I assure him.

"Can I see it?" he asks.

"Sure," I answer.

EVIL SUSPECTS

1. **Emilio**
2. **Emilio**
3. **Emilio**
4. **Emilio**
5. **Emilio**
6. **Emilio**

"I'm every name on the list," says Emilio.

"That might be a typo," I answer.

"That doesn't seem likely."

"Yes, well, forgive me. My Arctic secretary has fled to Cuba, and I'm not good at typing. There are more suspects on the other page."

MORE EVIL SUSPECTS

1. **Lighthouse Larry**
2. **Speedo Steve**
3. **Bongo Billy**
4. **My own mother**
5. **Various chickens**
6. **The man in the white hat**

"What man in the white hat?" asks Emilio.

"I don't know," I answer. "I just always list him."

"What about Bruce?" asks Emilio.

"Who the heck is that?"

"Captain Largo Spargo," he says.

"Oh, him. Can't be him."

"Why not?"

"He likes bran muffins."

BRAN MUFFIN

"So?"

"So that means he's a good person."

"That makes no sense."

"Because you know nothing about detective work."

"Fine. Then maybe it's Uncle Dave," says Emilio. "Because I know for a fact that he doesn't like bran muffins."

"Absurd," I cry.

"Why is that absurd?"

"Because Dave wants me to like him. Badly. And he knows that if he committed such an evil deed, I would curse his name to the heavens forevermore."

And with that, I look to the heavens.

And see a plane, high out over the ocean, skywriting.

...HI, EES ME, TOTAL, EEN PLANE...

It is my polar bear, no doubt seeking to make amends for his prior behavior.

And I am suddenly reassured.

ME GONNA DOO BOOKKS REEPORT...

And then less assured.

JUSS NEED HUNRED DOLLAR FOR MORE CHEEKEN...

And then even less assured.

UH-OH. ME JUSS DROPP BOOKKS EEN OCEAN...

CHAPTER
33
Good Night to the Iguana

It is getting dark as we walk home. And the walk is long.

"Let's cut through the old Key West cemetery," I tell my unpaid intern. "It will shave a couple of blocks off the walk."

Emilio stares at the headstones, many of them old and crumbling.

"C'mon," I say as he stops at the entrance.

But he doesn't move.

"Don't tell me you're afraid *again*," I tell him. "These people are dead, Emilio. It's not like they're gonna rise from the grave."

"I'm not going in there, Timmy."

"Emilio Empanada, you can't be afraid of *everything* in life. It's annoying. And it looks very bad on a job application."

"I don't care," he says. "I just want to go home."

So I climb onto one of the old headstones, marked WILSON.

"Fear must never hold a detective back," I remind my unpaid intern.

But he doesn't answer.

"Because," I continue, "as that famous quote says, 'If you are determined to succeed in life, nothing can stop you. Except maybe a truck.'"

I look around at the graves below me.

"Which may have hit some of these people."

My inspirational speech over, I glance back at Emilio.

But he is not there.

For he is already halfway home.

And as I begin climbing back down from the headstone, I feel a stirring from deep inside the tomb.

Someone rising from the grave.

And it is not Wilson. But an iguana.

And I leave to join my intern.

CHAPTER 34
Fee Largo

"What do you mean we can't go on the boat?" I yell at Largo Spargo as the sun peeks over the horizon. "My intern and I got up very early for this!"

"Well, first off, you only have a hundred dollars," says the captain.

"That was all the lamps we could sell," replies Emilio. "Er, books, I mean."

"And second," the captain continues, "you two are kids. You can't come onto the boat without a parent or guardian."

"We can't bring a *parent*!" I object. "That would compromise the integrity of our whole investigation! And besides, you never said anything about bringing a parent when we talked to you last time!"

"Sorry," says the captain as he unties his boat from the pier. "I figured you knew."

"Now what are we supposed to do?" asks Emilio.

So I contemplate what we can do.

I SHOULD HAVE LET YOU ON THE BOOOOOOAT....

"Something *legal* we can do," adds Emilio.

"Well, in that case, my plan is different," I answer.

"What is it?"

"We can start digging."

CHAPTER
35
Wasting Away Again in Marge and Rita-Ville

"Why do we have to dig so deep?" asks Emilio Empanada. "I'm tired. And I want to go swimming with Dinky Duck."

So I squeeze the life out of Dinky Duck.

FSSSHH

"You have to blow that back up," says Emilio.

"Fine," I answer. "When we're done."

"When are we done?"

"When we find it."

"When we find what?"

"When we find the treasure!" I snap.

"We're never gonna find treasure."

I throw my shovel to the ground and pull Emilio close.

"Emilio Empanada, there is treasure somewhere on this island. A whole lot of it. So much so that some captain wants to kill me over it. Now it may be in the water or it may be on land. But wherever it is, we are going to find it and stash it all in our new super-hidden global headquarters!"

"Fort Taylor?" asks Doorman Dave.

"Is there no privacy on this island?!" I cry.

"Sorry," says Dave. "It's just that I saw

you guys walking there. You can see it from our house."

"That does it," I announce. "We're moving our headquarters to Cuba. Emilio, start swimming."

Emilio starts swimming.

"Come back here," says Dave.

Emilio comes back here.

"You boys need to stop digging for a minute and have some lunch. I bought you both some Cubano sandwiches. Pork and ham on pressed bread. Delicious."

"Sounds wonderful," says Emilio, tucking a paper napkin into the top of his bathing suit.

"I have digging to do," I answer. "And I can get all the Cubano sandwiches I want when I get to Cuba. That is, if there's any food left."

"You'd leave Key West and give up on the captain's treasure here?" asks Dave.

I stare at him, dumbfounded.

"Sorry," he says. "You talk loud."

"First off," I answer, "I deny everything. Second, my agency's business is none of your concern, Dave. And third, we may have to shoot you."

"It's not personal," adds Emilio, patting Dave on the back. "It's just that it's top secret."

"I understand," says Doorman Dave. "I just thought that if you were looking for treasure, you'd want to know about Captain Tuft. Or maybe you already do. It's a pretty well-known story around here."

I toss my shovel to the side.

"If this is a ruse, you are doomed," I tell him.

"It's no ruse," says Dave.

"Then begin speaking," I tell him. "But remember, your fate may hang in the balance."

"Well, there's not much to say, really," explains Dave, pouring fried plantains onto his paper plate. "Atticus Tuft was a famous wrecker from the nineteenth century."

"A wrecker?" asks Emilio.

"Yeah, a wrecker," answers Dave. "You know, when ships used to get stuck on the reefs, wreckers were the people who would go out there and take all the valuables."

"I know all about history," I tell Dave. "You don't need to educate me."

"Well, great, then. So you know what he did with the loot?" asks Dave.

"I know everything," I answer. "But tell Emilio. He's still an unpaid intern."

"Yeah. Tell me," says Emilio, neatly

spreading mustard onto his Cubano sandwich.

"Well, people say the old captain stashed it somewhere on the island. And he never came back to get it."

"Why not?" asks Emilio.

"Two women," says Dave.

"Dames," I add. "It's always dames."

"Their names were Rita and Marge," continues Dave. "He loved them both. And when Rita found out about Marge, she wasn't very happy. So she poisoned the old captain's rum."

"He died?" asks Emilio.

"Yep," answers Dave. "Wasted away and died."

"And so nobody knows where he left the treasure?" asks Emilio.

"Nope," replies Dave.

"I do," I answer. "Follow me."

CHAPTER
36
The Throes of Kilimanjaro

"What is the most feared creature on earth?" I ask Emilio as we run down the sidewalk in our bathing suits.

"Where are we going?" replies Emilio.

"Never mind that," I answer. "What's the most feared creature on earth?"

"Lions."

"No."

"Tigers?"

"No."

"Bears?"

"Oh, my," I answer. *"Think."*

"I don't know," he says. "But can we please stop running? My stomach is filled with that Cubano sandwich. I think it's about to explode."

"Only one more block," I answer. "Now concentrate. What's the most feared creature on earth?"

"I don't know," says Emilio, holding his stomach.

"The butterfly!" I shout. "What else?"

"The butterfly?" replies Emilio. "Timmy, nobody fears butterflies."

"Wrong!" I answer. "Butterflies come from worms. And everyone hates worms!"

"Butterflies don't come from worms. They come from caterpillars."

"There is no difference. Both are slimy and long."

"So is a garden hose," says Emilio. "But that doesn't turn into a butterfly."

DOES NOT BECOME BUTTERFLY

"Will you please focus?" I lecture Emilio. "We're here."

BUTTERFLY CONSERVATORY

"A butterfly conservatory? Timmy, what does this have to do with anything?"

"Oh, good gosh. I know you're an intern, but don't you get anything?"

"Yes, I get an upset stomach when you make me run after eating a Cubano sandwich."

"No, Emilio Empanada. *Focus.* If you were a captain with the biggest treasure on the island of Key West, where would you hide it?"

"In a Key West bank."

"In a butterfly conservatory!" I shout. "Where it'd be safe! Because nobody wants to get eaten alive by butterflies! And nobody but a fearless detective would go inside."

And thus, we burst into the conservatory.

Or rather, I do.

"What are you doing?" I ask, poking my head back outside through the thick rubber strips that keep the butterflies from escaping.

"I'll be in there in a minute," says Emilio.

"Don't tell me you're afraid *again*."

"Of a butterfly?" mutters Emilio. "That's one thing I'm definitely *not* afraid of."

"Then what is it?"

"All that running on a full stomach. I think I'm gonna throw up."

A gurgling sound erupts from his mouth, like Mount Kilimanjaro ready to blow.

So he rushes into the bathroom.

And I rush in to see the butterflies.

And as soon as I am inside, I spot a little girl.

Being eaten alive.

And it is a horror to behold.

So I pass carefully by her.

"Hey, you—do you want a butterfly?" she asks as I pass.

"A what?" I ask, startled by the voice of the doomed soul.

"Hold your arm out and we'll see if I can get one of these little guys to fly onto you."

Oh, good God, I think. She is dead already, and like a zombie risen from the grave, her only satisfaction is in destroying other humans.

"You will do nothing of the kind!" I assert as I pass.

And as I do, there is a tiny itch-like crawl upon the top of my head.

And I look up.

And see my brains are being eaten.

"Timmy?" Emilio asks as he emerges from the bathroom. "Are you oka

CHAPTER 36 AND A HALF

THE END OF THE LAST
CHAPTER WAS CROSSED
OUT BY ME.
WITH MY OWN PEN.
IN EVERY SINGLE COPY OF
THIS BOOK THAT EXISTS.

(YOU CAN CHECK THEM ALL.
I WAS VERY THOROUGH.)
AND I DID IT BECAUSE THE
ENDING TO THE CHAPTER WAS
WRITTEN BY EMILIO EMPANADA,
WHO FELT THAT MY ORIGINAL
ENDING WAS NOT
              ACCURATE.

THUS, HE ASKED THE PUBLISHERS ~~IF HE COULD WRITE HIS OWN.~~ ~~AND THEY MALICIOUSLY AGREED.~~ ~~WHAT FOLLOWED WAS A~~ <u>HIGHLY</u> <u>INACCURATE</u> ~~VERSION OF EVENTS~~ ~~CONCERNING MY REACTION TO THE~~ ~~BUTTERFLY THAT LANDED ON~~ MY HEAD.

~~WHEREIN EMILIO SAID THAT I~~ ~~WAS SO SCARED, I CRIED.~~

~~I HAVE NEVER BEEN SCARED.~~ <u>AND I HAVE NEVER CRIED.</u>

SO I FOUND EVERY SINGLE COPY OF THIS BOOK AND CROSSED ALL THAT OUT.

AND PRESENT FOR YOU HERE
THE CORRECT ENDING TO
THAT CHAPTER:

TIMMY WAS
NOBLE AND
BRAVE.

CHAPTER 37

Conched Out Again

We are asked to leave the conservatory by an employee who says that we are creating a disturbance.

Emilio blames me.

I blame Emilio.[2]

The only thing we agree upon is what happened next.

Which is that when we got home, we found something on our porch.

---

2. I am right. He is wrong.

With a poem inside.

FROM ON HIGH
I'M THE GUY
WITH A SHIP
IN HIS GRIP
GO AWAY
OR YOU'LL PAY
'COS THE BRAVE
EARN THE GRAVE

RIP

CHAPTER
38
One Fish, Two Fish,
Dead Fish, Blue Fish

"I think Dr. Seuss is trying to kill us," I tell Emilio.

"No, Timmy," answers Emilio.

"He's the only guy who can rhyme like that."

"No."

"It's a shame, too. Because I was a big fan of *One Fish Two Fish*. And now he wants me dead."

"Timmy, it's not Dr. Seuss," he says, pacing the porch.

I hold the conch shell to my ear.

"Hey, Emilio, I can hear the ocean. It's saying, 'Emilio Empanada knows nothing about detective work.'"

"Yes, well, I know that conch shells don't talk."

"This one does."

"Terrific. Then what's it say we should do next?"

"Raise money. Lots of it. For more cannons. Tanks. And perhaps dolphins."

"Dolphins?"

"Yes. So we can ride them from island to island."

"Speaking of money," says Emilio, "do we still have that hundred dollars we were gonna use for the boat?"

"No. It's been sent to Cuba," I answer. "I've been the victim of an outrageous extortion scheme."

TELEGRAM

TIMMY
KEEY WST
GOT MONEES - (STOP) - ALMOSS DUN
BOOKK REEPORT - (STOP) - ME UNLY
FEENISH IF YOO MAKE ME PARDNER
IN DEETECTIF AGECY - (STOP) -
ME FATT NOW - (STOP) -
TOTAL

"Oh, no," says Emilio.

"Yes," I answer. "My polar bear is trying to extort me into making him a named partner in my detective agency. He is an evil fiend."

"I see."

"But extortion or no extortion, we are running out of time. And my precious life hangs in the balance. So we cannot let the investigation be hindered."

But the investigation is immediately hindered.

By the person who always hinders.

"Timmy, I need you to get dressed," says my mom. "Your clothes are on the bed. They're new, so I hope they fit."

"New clothes? What now?"

"We have to meet someone."

"Who?" I ask.

"Let's talk about it inside."

CHAPTER 39

Please, Mr. Postman, Look at Timmy

My mom talked forever.

And she was weird and made me hold her hand and sometimes she seemed sad.

But I'm a detective. And we don't have feelings.

At least not ones we show.

So I'm gonna keep this short.

The person we have to meet is my dad.

"I had to call him to let him know I was getting remarried," she said. "Then he asked some questions. And I happened to mention that we were going to Key West for the honeymoon. And it turns out he's been living in the Keys. And he'd like to say hi to you."

And on and on she went.

Telling me I've met him before.

Telling me I used to call him Papa.

Telling me he may or may not show up.

Now I know I haven't said much about him before, or even mentioned him.

But there are reasons for that.

All of which are contained in this memo.

From deep within the Timmy files.

MEMO TO FILE

SUBJECT: DAD

MOM SAYS MY DAD LEFT
BEFORE I WAS BORN.

THAT'S BECAUSE HE'S AN
INTERNATIONAL SECRET AGENT.

WHO HAS CAUGHT CRIMINALS
IN ALMOST ALL THE
COUNTRIES ON EARTH.

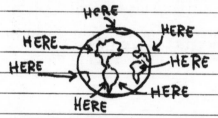

HE IS, TO MANY IN THE LAW
ENFORCEMENT COMMUNITY, A
SUPERHERO.

AND LIKE THE SUPERHERO HE
IS, HE CAN SCALE BUILDINGS
WITH ONE HAND:

(LIKE THIS)

AND STOP TRAINS WITH THE OTHER:

AND WRESTLE WHALES:

AND EAT ALL OF THE SUPER BURRITO
AT SAM'S SUPER BURRITO.

BUT HIS WORK IS SO DANGEROUS
THAT HE CANNOT COME HOME.
FOR HIS ENEMIES EXPECT HIM
THERE.

EXCEPT FOR ONE CHRISTMAS.
WHEN I WAS TOO YOUNG
    TO REMEMBER.

BUT ASSASSINS ATTACKED.
AND HE HAD TO FLEE UP
    THE CHIMNEY.

BLOCKING THE ENTIRE CHIMNEY.
ANGERING MY MOTHER.
AND PREVENTING SANTA
    FROM DELIVERING PRESENTS.

AND HE CAN'T SEND LETTERS.

BECAUSE LETTERS REQUIRE A RETURN ADDRESS.

AND IF HE WROTE THAT DOWN, THE CRIMINALS COULD FIND HIM.

And that's all I can share about my dad.

The international secret agent.

Because that's how he'd want it.

Which I understand.

Because I have his genes.

And now his attention.

CHAPTER 40
Papa's House

My mother wants to stay and sit with me and my father on the bench outside the dead author's house.

But I tell her to leave.

For I am being pursued by assassins, and, doubtless, so is my father.

"It's dangerous enough as it is," I tell her. "This is no place for civilians."

So she leaves and walks back inside the author's house.

And I sit down with my dad.

"I won't keep you long," he says. "I know it's a bit awkward. And your mom wasn't thrilled with any of this anyway."

"The cats here stole my pants," I reply.

"Yes. I see that."

"Hold on to yours," I warn him.

"I will."

"Good. They are all remorseless criminals."

We both stare at the cats.

"I guess I owe you an explanation for everything," he says.

"No need," I tell him. "I understand. I'm a law-enforcement officer myself."

"Ah, yes. Your mom told me all about your

many investigations. And the notes from your friend—"

"Emilio. He's my intern."

"Yes, Emilio."

We watch a six-toed cat pass. I hang on to my wallet.

"Let me just say something, Tim—" He pauses. "Do you like 'Tim' or 'Timmy'?"

"Timmy."

"Let me just say something, Timmy."

"Okay. You talk. I'll scan the bushes for assassins."

ASSASSIN

"It's just that running a business down here in the Keys is hard. I wouldn't expect you to understand any of this, but it's a little hole-in-the-wall restaurant, you know? That's what

I own. And you have to be there about twenty hours a day. For real."

I smile, appreciating his cover story. A hole-in-the-wall restaurant—that's a good one.

"'Cos with a restaurant, if you're not there, I tell you, you really get robbed blind by your employees. The bartenders steal. The waitresses steal. Everyone steals."

"I understand," I tell him. "Remember, I had my pants stolen."

He smiles.

"Anyhow, Tim—Timmy—that stupid place takes up all my time, and it's why I can't come see you as often as I'd like or call as often, you know?"

"I understand. It would be a great risk."

"Well, I don't know about that."

"It would. It'd be dangerous."

He laughs. "You mean, your mom yelling at me for not coming around enough? Maybe."

We both know I'm talking about the criminals that pursue him relentlessly. But they could be eavesdropping from the eaves.

EAVESDROPPING FROM THE EAVES

And thus I play along with my dad's cover story.

"I understand everything," I assure him.

"I dunno," he says. "I think I have too many excuses. Anyhow, maybe I should just let you ask me something instead of me going on and on about everything."

I watch a group of tourists pass. And then turn back to my dad.

"Have you heard about my work?" I ask.

"Your schoolwork? Your mom tells me a little."

"Schoolwork? Pshaw. My detective work. You know, in your community."

He laughs.

"Why are you laughing?"

He stops.

"Gee, Timmy, I don't know much of anything. You know, I work all the time."

"I see. Well, the agency is the best of its kind. And it's growing rapidly."

"Ah. I see."

We're interrupted by a man with a large belly and a visor. "Excuse me, do you know where Hemingway's studio is? The place where he wrote?"

"I've only been here once," says my dad. "But I think it's at the back. Up the stairs."

"That was frightening," I whisper to my

father as the man lumbers off. "I thought it was an ambush."

"Nope," says my dad. "He was just lost."

And half smiles.

"I came here once when I was a young man myself," says my dad. "Wanted to be Hemingway. Write novels, you know? Spy novels, mysteries. Never was any good. Nothing published or anything. Never tried, really. But anyhow, that's all in the past."

I nod, amazed at the depths of his cover story.

"Anyhow, to make this short, Timmy, I just want to say I'm sorry. I know I'm not the greatest dad. Not much of a dad at all, really. I mean, I know it's no excuse, but my own dad barely spent any time with me at all, and I had you when I was so young, and I was scared and I didn't know what I was doing and—"

"Mom says that one time she had to pay for a private school for me," I interrupt him, "and she asked you for money and you didn't give her any."

"Really?"

"Yes."

"Well, I probably just didn't have it at the time. But if I had it, I would have sent it."

"Okay."

"I don't even remember that, to be honest."

"I do," I answer.

My mother raps on the window of the Hemingway house and points at her watch.

"She's always interrupting," I explain.

"Yeah, well, that probably means we have to wrap things up," says my dad.

"Okay."

There is a long pause.

"I'll be better, Tim. Better dad. The whole bit."

"Yeah."

"I will."

"Okay."

"And I'm real proud of you."

"Okay."

We stand. Silent for a moment. Then we shake hands.

"You be good," he says.

"Don't let the cats steal your wallet," I answer.

CHAPTER
41
The Short Happy Life
of Timmy the Detective

"I've been thinking a lot about what that poem means," says Emilio as he plays with Edward Higglebottom the Third back at the rental house. "The one in the conch shell."

"I haven't," I answer.
"Why not?"

"Because I don't care."

"What are you talking about?"

"I just want to go home," I answer. "I'm tired of this place."

"Tired of it? What about all the notes?"

"I don't care. It's hot here. And I want to sleep in my own bed again."

"Well, we can't leave before solving the mystery."

"Emilio, there are some mysteries that just can't be solved. It happens sometimes."

"But I want to solve it."

"Yes, well, you're not going to, okay?"

"But why not?"

"Because it's over. Your internship. The mystery. The whole thing."

Emilio puts the baby chicken back in his cardboard box.

"And besides," I add, "the trip's almost done anyway."

He stares at his suitcase.

"We're leaving tomorrow?" he asks.

"Tomorrow," I answer.

"Then I guess I should probably start packing."

He picks up a shirt and rolls it up like a sleeping bag.

"Prevents wrinkles," he says.

He repeats the process with his pants and his shorts and even his underwear until his suitcase is filled.

A model of uptight organization.

Then he sits down on his bed.

"I heard that you saw your dad," he says.

"Yes, well, we're not talking about that. It was a profound waste of time."

"Okay," he says.

And rolls up another shirt.

"I was raised by my aunt," he says.

I look over at my intern.

"You were what?" I ask.

"My aunt. She raised me."

"You didn't say anything about that."

"I know. I don't talk about it a lot."

I loosen the dumb tie that my mother made me wear.

"Why'd you have to be raised by her?" I ask.

"Dunno," he says. "I guess she's the one who wanted to do it. Or could. Or something."

"Oh," I answer. "Well, that was nice of her, I guess."

"Yeah. She's very nice. A little strict. But nice."

I take my tie off and throw it on the floor.

"So that's where you live now?" I ask. "With your aunt?"

He nods. "Well, I spend most of the year with her and part of the year with my uncle."

"Doorman Dave?"

"Yeah. Doorman Dave." He laughs. "He's the one who takes me to all the fun places during the summer."

"This place is hardly fun," I remind him.

"I've liked it," he says. "It's been exciting. Going to the beach. Spending time with you. Raising money for the investigation."

He smiles.

"I was even thinking about what piece of furniture we could sell next," he adds.

And as he says it, I hear loud footsteps thundering down the bedroom hallway.

So I peer outside.

And see this:

"You're stealing our furniture to raise money for more chicken dinners!" I cry.

But my polar bear doesn't answer.

He just turns and flees.

And I am too tired to chase him.

So I walk back into the bedroom and lie down.

"Sell whatever you want," I tell Emilio. "I just don't care."

And I roll over.

And fall asleep.

CHAPTER
42
May the Good Lord Shine
a Lighthouse on You

When I wake up the next day, the room is empty.

Except for Edward Higglebottom the Third, who is out of his box and dangerously close to my nose.

"Is there nowhere safe on this entire island?" I cry.

So I throw on my clothes and leave the house.

Wanting nothing more than for time to pass so I can leave this stupid place.

And thus I wander the streets.

Eventually arriving at the author's house where I met my father.

And I sit on the bench.

Alone.

And hear a scream from the sky.

"TIIIIIIIIIIIIIIIIIIIIIIIIIIMMMMMMMM-MMY!"

So I look up.

And there, at the top of the lighthouse across the street, is my unpaid intern.

"Hiya!" he yells. "I hope you don't mind, but I had to sell your shoes to get up here. The ones you wore with your fancy clothes."

"Emilio Empanada, what are you doing way up there?" I shout from the base of the lighthouse.

"Trying not to be afraid of everything," he answers. "Which isn't easy. Because I'm still afraid."

And even from a distance, I can see his knees shaking.

"Remember how you said that if you're determined to succeed in life, nothing can stop you?" he shouts.

"Except maybe a truck," I add.

"Yeah, well, I thought everyone should know that. But I didn't have quite enough room for the whole quote. So I shortened it a bit."

"What are you talking about?" I yell up at him.

"Follow me."

He walks to the opposite side of the lighthouse.

And I follow him around and look up.

It is the first time I have seen my name displayed so prominently in a public forum.

"I wrote it in chalk so that I can't get arrested or anything. Plus, Bongo Billy said it was okay."

I stare in awe at my own name, writ large across the city skyline.

"You may erase two demerits," I proudly tell my intern. "Perhaps even three."

"Oh, and that's not all," he adds.

"What else?" I shout up at him.

Emilio disappears into the interior of the lighthouse.

And appears again at the bottom.

"I think I solved the mystery."

CHAPTER 43

Atticus! Atticus!

Emilio runs through the streets holding a shovel high overhead.

"What do you need that for?" I ask, sprinting behind him.

"For the treasure! I think I know where it is."

I am immediately skeptical. For the

number of mysteries solved through the ages by an unpaid intern is exactly:

"Start explaining," I yell at him as I run. "And keep in mind that you are talking to a seasoned professional."

"The clues are all in the poem!" Emilio says as he runs. "'From on high I'm the guy.'"

"What about it?"

"'With a ship in his grip'!"

"I know the dumb poem!" I remind my intern.

"But I saw him!" shouts Emilio. "From the top of the lighthouse!"

"Who?"

"The guy with the ship in his grip! It's a big statue. It was impossible to miss!"

"Yes, well, I would have seen it first if you had allowed me the proper amount of time up there!"

He ignores me and darts down a narrow street filled with old homes and large palm trees.

"It was somewhere near here," he says. "Just past that last house."

Emilio races to the end of the block.

Confident. Brave.

And confronting his fears.

And turning the corner, he finds where the statue is located.

And must now confront one more.

ATTICUS
TUFT
1835-1876

R.I.P.

CHAPTER 44

The Ecstasy of the Bold

Emilio stares at the graveyard, silent as the graves themselves.

But for his eyes.

Which slowly scan from one crumbling end of the graveyard to the other.

"My aunt raised me because my parents are in heaven," he says.

Not looking back at me.

"I was a baby," he adds. "I don't remember them."

I put my hand on his shoulder.

"You don't have to go in if you don't want to," I tell him.

"I know," he says, motionless.

"We can just go home," I remind him.

"I know."

And with that, he turns and walks back to the cemetery gates.

"Fear," he says, his back turned to me.

"Fear is okay," I tell him.

"Fear," he repeats.

"It's okay."

"Fear," he says again, turning to face me, "must never hold a detective back."

And he runs.

Into the graveyard.

Past the headstones.

Over the graves.

Like a rabbit let loose from its cage.

"'Cos the brave earn the grave!" he yells as he runs. "'Cos the brave earn the grave!"

And I chase after him.

"It's not a threat, Timmy! *It's a reward!*"

And he is right.

For the brave do earn the grave.

And there before us is our reward.

ATTICUS
TUFT
1835-1876

CHAPTER 45

One Grand

"Dig!" he shouts, handing me the shovel. "I'll watch for assassins!"

So I slice into the fresh dirt.

And as I do, the grave slithers and stirs.

And I am once again face-to-face with the Green Monster of Doom.

So I glance over at Emilio.

And back at my foe.

And then I do this:

Scaring the beast.

And clearing the grave.

And raising the shovel high overhead, I thrust it into the soft dirt.

And I dig.

And I dig.

And I dig.

And there, a few inches below the surface, I hit something.

"The treasure!" shouts Emilio.

"An envelope," I answer.

"Is it gold coins?"

"I can't feel any," I reply, patting down the outside of it.

"Well, open it!" he yells.

So I open it.

And find a piece of paper.

"This is no captain's treasure!" I shout. "It's just a stupid piece of paper."

"Let me see," says Emilio, grabbing it from my hands.

"You can have it," I tell him. "It's worth-less."

So Emilio examines the document.

And hands it back to me.

"It's not worthless, Timmy. It's a college savings bond. And it's got your name on it."

"A college savings what?" I ask.

"Bond."

"What the heck is that?"

"I think it helps you pay for college one day. And it's for a thousand dollars."

I grab the piece of paper back.

"A thousand dollars? Who would want to pay a thousand dollars for me to go to college?"

And as I say it, I see the answer to my own question.

Printed neatly in the corner of the savings bond.

CHAPTER 46

For Whom the Dumb Videophone Tolls Again

I walk home, securely clutching the captain's treasure to my chest.

I think about thanking my father with a telegram.

But he's an international secret agent.

And I wouldn't know where to send it.

And besides, secret agents don't have time to answer.

Because fighting crime is a full-time job.

As I am reminded when I enter our kitchen.

And see the worst thing a human being can ever see:

So I grab the cereal box and prepare to dump its contents on the floor.

"Hey," says Doorman Dave, seated at the table, "I'm eating that."

I stare at Dave.

And put the box back on the table.

"Sorry, Dave," I tell him. "Enjoy your cold cereal. It's the least a man can have on his honeymoon."

"Thanks, Timmy."

And I look back at the laptop and see that we are all still exposed to the evil that is Corrina Corrina.

So I slam the laptop shut as she talks.

"Did your room just go dark or something?" asks Corrina Corrina.

"Yes, we had a power outage," I inform her. "And I know you're calling to harass me about the book report, and you can be assured it will be done—"

"Beautifully!" she ends my sentence.

"Beautifully?" I ask.

"Yeah, it was e-mailed to me. It's amazing. So much detail. You really understood those books, Timmy."

I think of my polar bear. And his limited skill set.

"Was the spelling okay?" I ask. "It didn't sound like Tarzan or something? You know, like 'Me want . . . Me need . . . Me eat'?"

Corrina Corrina laughs. "You're being silly," she says. "Anyhow, good work." And ends the call.

And as she does, my mom hands me the house phone.

"Another call for Mr. Popular," she says. "But don't talk too long. We have to finish packing."

I grab the phone. "Hello?" I say.

And on the other end I hear the voice of Abraham Lincoln.

Who is no longer Abraham Lincoln.

JUST
ROLLO
NOW

Stanfurd

"The play was canceled," says Rollo, sounding disappointed. "The stage curtain had to be dry-cleaned."

"So?" I ask.

"Well, I had nothing else to do, so I just went ahead and did your book report."

I stand there silent, in awe of my noble, round friend.

"I owe you, Rollo Tookus. Rest assured, you will be given an ownership stake in my detective agency just as soon as we issue shares."

"That's okay," he says. "I actually like doing book reports."

"Okay, well, that's weird. But I like you anyway."

"Okay," he says. "I'll see you when you get home tomorrow."

"Yeah," I answer. "And Rollo . . ."

"What?" he asks.

"Thank you."

CHAPTER 47

Across the Highway and Into the Grass

There is not much left to say.

Except that I might be spending a lot more time with Emilio Empanada.

"My aunt says it would be fine if me and Edward Higglebottom the Third spent more time with you and your mom and Dave!" he tells me on the long drive home. "Maybe the whole summer."

"That's good," I tell him. "As there may be a paid position opening up in the detective agency."

"Why is that?"

"Because I've been contacted by my polar bear. And I may have to fire him for incompetence."

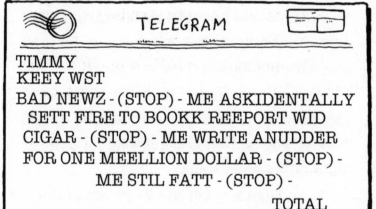

TELEGRAM

TIMMY
KEEY WST
BAD NEWZ - (STOP) - ME ASKIDENTALLY SETT FIRE TO BOOKK REEPORT WID CIGAR - (STOP) - ME WRITE ANUDDER FOR ONE MEELLION DOLLAR - (STOP) - ME STIL FATT - (STOP) -

TOTAL

And as I finish talking, my mother takes a call on her cell phone.

"Timmy," she says, leaning back over the

front seat, "do you by chance know anything about missing furniture at the rental house?"

"Why are you asking me?"

"Because that was the owner of the house we rented. She says they're missing stuff."

I look over at Emilio.

And then back at my mother.

"You should never have let Corrina Corrina see the inside of our house," I tell her. "Sounds like the poor girl robbed us blind."

My mother shakes her head at me and goes back to talking on the cell phone.

And as she argues about rental deposits and missing furniture, Dave pulls the car off the highway and into the parking lot of a gas station convenience store.

"Last chance to get snacks for about thirty miles," says Dave.

I don't want any, so I stand outside the store, in the middle of nowhere, as Emilio and Dave go inside.

And when Emilio comes back out, there is a large soda stain on the front of his shirt.

"That's okay," says Emilio. "It's just a dumb shirt."

I smile, proud of my intern's emotional progress.

And as we wait for Dave, I walk to the edge of the parking lot and stare out at the endless landscape of high grass.

Aware of the infinite possibilities that await us.

And as I do, I feel a tiny itch-like crawl upon the top of my head.

And

AND TIMMY WAS
NOBLE AND BRAVE.

THE END

STEPHAN PASTIS is the creator of the *New York Times* bestselling Timmy Failure series, the first of which was a 2014 BookTrust Best Book Awards winner, a runner-up in the 2014 Sainsbury's Children's Book Awards and listed as one of 100 Children's Modern Classics by *The Sunday Times*. He is also the creator of *Pearls Before Swine*, an acclaimed comic strip that appears in more than seven hundred newspapers and boasts a devoted following. Stephan lives in northern California, USA.